The Mage's Code

a novel by Daniel P. Mayer

Directory

"Whenever magic returns to prominence, I fear that he will return to punish us."

- K. L.

Being a phantom is one of those things you just start to take for granted after a while. As the world passes you by, the days blending together into the weeks, into the months and years beyond, all without a human soul ever noticing you, you just sort of fall into a rhythm that happens almost unconsciously. I had some trouble getting used to meeting, or rather avoiding, the glances of strangers as I walked the streets. While I vaguely remembered a handful of social niceties I could employ, I preferred to save them until they were absolutely necessary.

The man I found myself seeking out for asylum at least could relate somewhat to my experience. Living on the street will condition a man to expect passersby to stop noticing him, as if he were already in the grip of death and not merely close to its doorstep. I never bothered to learn this man's name. He fit every stereotype you might imagine of a man living on the street, with perhaps the exception of a pair of faded denim suspenders, and a tattered camouflage hat with some sort of military insignia on it. As I approached him, he only made a modest effort to conceal the paper bag he had cradled beside him, tucking it under his coat and sitting up straight against the brick wall he currently occupied.

"Well now, what do you call this getup?" he said, looking me up and down. "You some kind of re-enactor or whatever they're called?"

I just stared at him for a moment. My conversational skills were similarly out of practice, not that they were ever truly top-notch. I would've liked to think I learned from the best, though.

"Perhaps you haven't heard," I replied finally, tipping my faded bowler hat to him. "Fashion is cyclical. What's old is new again. I myself can hardly wait until the sixties make their comeback. If I encourage ladies to burn their bras now, I get the strangest looks."

The older man laughed, his laugh transitioning into a raspy cough.

"Well young fella, I sure hate to ask something like this, seeing as my daddy didn't raise me to be asking for handouts from anybody, but as it is, I'm a long way off from my family downstate, and if you-"

"Yes yes, I've heard all of this before." I cut him off with an aloof wave of the hand. "You're a good Christian man, your daddy raised you better than this, you never wanted to take advantage of the kindness of strangers, but couldn't I please find it in my heart to spare a few dollars to help an old crippled veteran pay for his bus fair? I have seen you deliver various versions of this speech numerous times. While I must respect your craft as an actor, I'm afraid the writing loses a little something in repeated viewings."

"H-hey now! I ain't a liar. My hand to God, son, I-"

"Please, spare me the theatrics."

I reached into my pocket and pulled out a wad of crumpled bills, and handed the entire pile to him.

"I don't care whether you served in any war, or if your legs work or not. I just need a bit of your time, and I'm perfectly content to pay you for it."

The man was taken aback, but gradually reached forward and took the money, seemingly expecting me to snatch it away at any moment. With some incredulity, he realized he was holding at least several hundred dollars.

"What in... I can't take all this. What is this, a trick? Somebody's looking for this money, is that it?"

"No tricks, I assure you. And the money does not belong to anyone who will notice it missing. This is simply a gesture of respect from one lonely soul to another."

"I... Oh, god bless you, son. Thank you so much. So, so much. You're a good man."

"I am nothing of the sort, and I resent any suggestion otherwise. Even so, I do hope this small gesture will be sufficient to initiate a mutually-beneficial friendship of sorts between the two of us."

The older man choked out another raspy laugh. "Son, today you are my best friend in the whole world."

"Excellent. Then I do hope you will heed this humble request from a friend. In the past, I have noticed you bringing money you've acquired from begging into the liquor store down the street, and surreptitiously exiting with bags containing the store's goods."

"Oh..." He sheepishly clambered to his feet, making less of an effort to conceal the bottle. "Is this the part where you tell me that I need to change my path and embrace the spirit of the lord's forgiveness or some such?"

"No, this is the part where I ask you to get blind drunk with me in broad daylight." He seemed at a loss for words at my response, so I continued. "I would like you to invite your friends from around the area to come and meet us in the park, go and buy as much alcohol as the proprietor will sell you, and together we'll raise a ruckus that will wake the dead."

"Hot damn. Why are you looking to do

something like that?"

"I need to spend the night in jail, and this seems to me the most straightforward and enjoyable means to attain that end."

The man scratched his head, looked at the wad of cash in his hand, and shrugged.

"Aw hell, why not? I ain't exactly got a lot of job interviews lined up. I know some guys down the way could use a night off the street, and lord knows the mission ain't giving them beds anymore. I gotta tell you though, it'll have to be one hell of a 'ruckus' to bring the police around this neighborhood. They ain't exactly in a big hurry to answer calls south of 25th street."

"Some of them might be. Which reminds me, actually. Pardon me one moment."

As my new friend, if he could be called that, gathered up his few possessions and started down the street to put my nefarious plan into action, I took out the small black notebook I always kept in my coat pocket, flipped to the first empty page and began writing, lest I should start to forget the chain of events which drove me to this ludicrous plan in the first place.

Don't underestimate the detective.

Chapter 1: The Detective

I felt pretty lucky to become a detective at such a young age. When my career started, I was still fresh out of school with a degree in Criminal Justice. I got a job in a precinct close to where I grew up. Watching detective dramas on TV might have set my expectations a little high as far as how exciting the day-to-day job would be. I got a badge and a gun, but for a couple of years, I was more or less a glorified secretary. I mostly handled record-keeping, preparing evidence for trials, and filing reports that my seniors didn't want to or didn't have time to deal with, because unlike me they actually went out and investigated active cases. I was stuck at my desk making sure all the I's were dotted and the T's were crossed. It was tedious business, but I guess everyone has to earn their place.

As I was doing my job, a lot of reports would come across my desk each day. A lot of them already had an arrest made by the time I got them, some were still ongoing investigations, and every once in a while I'd get the lost causes. Basically, these were cases where there were no leads left to investigate, or the crime was too insignificant to waste any more man-hours on: minor thefts, break-ins with no witnesses, and things like that. The reports would get filed away, and whoever committed the crimes would likely never be caught. I found those cases the most fascinating.

When I had some free time to spare, sometimes I would just sit and read some of those reports. As I looked them over, I would find myself trying to piece together what could have happened just for fun. I started getting a lot of weird hunches about people, their guilt or innocence. You can't make arrests on a hunch, but that wouldn't stop me from thinking about them, maybe too long in some cases.

I was walking to the station one morning, when I noticed a man walking a few yards in front of me. The old-fashioned bowler hat and trench coat he wore sort of stood out. Something about him gave me a weird slightly paranoid feeling, and I started following him a little more closely. As I looked at him, he turned his head and momentarily glanced back over his shoulder. He looked to be in his late twenties or early thirties, was clean shaved, and his blue-gray eyes wouldn't quite meet mine directly, as if hoping that I wouldn't notice him looking at me. I was sure I'd never met him before, but that paranoid feeling grew even stronger. It was the same feeling I get when I'm looking at a case and I think I have a hunch about who did it. Detective's intuition, I guess I would have called it, and it was throwing up a big red flag over this guy.

When I got to the street the station was on, without any hesitation, I walked right on by and kept following him. I never entertained my hunches this much, but I thought just this once couldn't hurt. If I caught crap for being a few minutes late, I figured I could blame the construction on Central. I followed him for another two and a half blocks, when he suddenly turned and went down an alley. That definitely struck me as odd, because I knew this street, and I knew that alley was a dead end. I followed suit and turned into the alley, only to find he'd just disappeared. I was sure I saw him walk into that alley seconds before I did, and yet the alley was empty. The one door he could have escaped through didn't open from the outside, and even if it could I was definitely close enough that I should have heard the door shut behind him. He hadn't gone inside. He was just gone.

I turned and headed back toward the station, trying to figure out what just happened. When I gave up making sense of a guy vanishing into thin air, I began mentally kicking myself for being so impulsive and irresponsible. Even if I had any reason to suspect he was up to no good, it was stupid to just follow him like that without a plan and without backup. Nothing had happened this time, and maybe I would've just been stalking an innocent man, but what if I had been right, and the guy had a gun or something? The whole idea was crazy anyway. I'd barely been out from behind my desk yet, and there I was blindly following would-be suspects. I wouldn't have even known what to do if I caught him.

Still, I kept trying to make sense of it, and why I was drawn to that guy in the first place. I thought maybe I'd just been paying attention because he looked out of place. In fact, I realized he reminded me of something I'd seen a few days earlier, in a report about a convenience store robbery.

When I got back to my desk, I took another look at that file. The report stated that about $80 worth of merchandise had disappeared from the shelves sometime in the evening. An employee had been the prime suspect, but there was no physical evidence pointing to him. Security camera footage didn't show anyone near the area where the items had been stolen, but the employee insisted he saw a customer back there acting suspiciously a little while before the store closed for the night. He described the customer as being about 5-foot-10, early to mid 30s, and wearing an "old-timey" black hat.

It wasn't anything concrete, but I was intrigued. I eagerly got through my usual work as quickly as possible, then started looking through the active cases for any of the usual lost causes. I kept following my hunch, and as I skimmed through file after file, I started seeing a pattern. There was a steady stream of cases where money and goods were stolen with no sign of a break-in and no evidence to go on. As I kept digging, I found a few more eyewitness accounts that mentioned a man in a black hat.

For weeks, I kept compiling evidence of what I perceived to be a crime spree: a serial burglar that somehow had always avoided detection. I didn't dare share this information with anyone at the station. I knew they'd think I was reading too much into things, that I was being obsessive. After a while, I was starting to think so myself. I even spotted him on the street a couple more times, only to watch him vanish from sight like a mirage as soon as I got closer. I started to wonder if I was chasing a ghost. For a little while I just kind of stopped snooping, but I still kept my eyes open for anything unusual.

My next break came after I got assigned a new case to help investigate. I had been putting in the hours and showing my senior officers I was competent, until finally my supervisor decided I was ready to work on active crime scenes, gathering evidence and taking statements from witnesses. I thanked him profusely for the opportunity and promised I'd do my best.

Later that day, I was in an old apartment building downtown following up on a string of burglaries. I had just taken a statement from a tenant when I caught sight of a familiar man in a black bowler hat walking down the hall. I turned to follow him. Finally, I had legitimate reason to approach him, and even in a relatively enclosed space where I might have a chance to catch him if he tried to run.

"Excuse me, sir?" I said, walking at a brisk pace to catch up to him. He didn't respond. "Sir? You, in the trench coat. Mind if I ask you a few questions?"

"Yes, I do." He kept walking without turning around, but I persisted.

"I'm Detective John Powers. Could I just have a moment of your time?"

"No, you could not."

"Sir, I'm here on official police business."

"That doesn't concern me."

I followed him closer, just a few steps behind. "What's the big hurry?"

He gave an annoyed sigh. "Listen, I just-"

"Have something to hide?" I cut him off. He turned back to look at me. If he recognized me, he didn't show it. He turned forward again and increased his pace as we got to the stairs. I sped up to match his pace, making sure I didn't lose sight of him, and he sped up again.

"Hey!"

We were both practically running down the stairs, but I was right on his heels. I reached out and grabbed him by the arm. He tried to pull away, but I held him tight. He whipped around and glared at me. His face had twisted into an angry sneer, but I could swear I saw a hint of fear in his eyes.

"Who the hell are you?"

I was surprised to hear *him* say what I was just about to.

"I just told you who I am," I replied, showing my badge with my free hand. "Now who are you?"

He kept his eyes fixed on mine, and his expression relaxed slowly. "I don't know what you're playing at, Detective. Nor do I have any interest in finding out."

He turned and threw himself over the railing, wrenching free of my grip as he fell. It was at least a twenty foot drop. I never heard him hit the floor. I looked over the railing but saw nothing. Just like that, he was gone again.

Naturally, nobody at the station was going to believe what happened. Even I didn't fully believe it. I just filed the report saying the suspect fled as soon as I tried to question him and managed to get away from me on the stairs. I mentioned the same details to the other investigator on the scene, and we continued to question people in the building. A few had seen him as well but nobody knew who the man was. The case remained open for a while, but no more leads turned up. Detectives were assigned to work on other cases.

I placed a copy of the report in my private unsolved file. I knew it wouldn't be the last time I saw him.

Chapter 2: The Ghost and The Madam

While I do enjoy drawing comparisons to phantoms or specters, they are ultimately misnomers for my state of being. I am not dead, nor have I ever been. Even with the benefits of my phantom form, more appropriately called my æthereal form, there are some trappings of mortal life I cannot fully escape from. I still require some nourishment from time to time, though even if I didn't require it, I would start to miss the sensation of eating and drinking after too long. Even relieving oneself brings a certain sense of... well, relief. In hindsight, that sensation is likely to be the entire reason behind this turn of phrase existing. The intricacies of language can be puzzling at times, so I am occasionally caught off-guard when etymology turns out to be so straightforward.

I seem to have meandered somewhat off of the point.

In addition to the previously mentioned bodily functions, I have found that sleep is completely impossible as an apparition. I suppose this is because it is a function of the living human body. If the choice were left to me, I would have generally preferred to remain eternally sleepless, but attempting to do so seems to have some detrimental effects on the mind, clouding thoughts and twisting memories into jagged thorny little things that become difficult to grasp. Besides which, eternity has a tendency to become boring after some time, so any quiet hours that can be given over to sleep, even fitful and restless sleep, seem well worth the investment.

All of this is to say that there is no avoiding the occasional need to become an ordinary flesh-and-blood human being from time to time. It's far from ideal, but with a minimal investment of time and observation, it becomes fairly easy to blend in among the regular folk long enough to acquire what I need, even if my clothing choices are not always appropriate for the setting.

Existing only for brief periods of time can make regular human existence difficult, however. In the modern era, it is rather difficult to obtain reliable employment without references, a place of residence, photo identification, or really any discernible proof that one does in fact exist. As such, I have had to make do stealing what I need to survive and sleeping in abandoned and condemned apartment buildings. It's a very simple way to subsist. Perhaps that's why it suits me so well.

My thefts have generally been minor and I tend not to take from the same locations again if the owners have suspected anything amiss. The police have no motivation to waste their time and resources on such minor crimes. Besides, I had an acquaintance in a position of power on the force who would guarantee most of my handiwork would not see any follow-up investigations. I had no reason to expect that any man with a badge would become a problem for me, yet that was exactly what had happened.

It was rather exciting, in a way. It had been a long time since I had any sort of real enemies to contend with. Here was a man who seemed to know my face, had some misguided desire to hold me accountable for my crimes, and even more surprising, escaping his grasp was not a trivial matter. At some point I would need to play detective myself to learn more about this young man, who he was, how much he knew, and just how potent his abilities were. He seemed unaware of what he was capable of at the time, but it was hard to know how long that ignorance might last.

Obviously, I needed some time to plan. I could not conduct my usual business in the same neighborhoods while this young detective was still poking his nose around. And so I was forced to wander elsewhere, which turned out to make quite a fateful difference.

As I drifted uptown, the scenery became less familiar by the moment. When I had some measure of privacy, I returned to human form in order to get a clearer picture of the area. Though I was obviously approaching the more affluent areas, and no doubt more fruitful grounds for the business of thievery, I noticed that while the buildings grew larger and more immaculate, they also seemed to be getting older, the styles of architecture scrolling backward through time as I passed by them.

One building in particular struck my fancy in an inexplicable way. By its size and opulent appearance, it could appropriately be described as a manor. A painted wooden sign at the front of the property declared this place to be the Lewis Museum, accompanying a nearby official placard from the city marking the building as a historical site. This placard described the building as having been passed down through several old and presumably tremendously wealthy families for over a century, until finally being renovated and opened to the public as a sort of cultural museum, educating locals on the rich history of their own hometown.

I had no special attachments I could speak of to

this place, but something about the museum struck me as intriguing. General admission was also free without a guided tour, which was a hard proposition to pass up even for someone like me.

"Welcome," a middle-aged man said as I walked through the main entrance. He was seated on a folding chair nearby, dwarfed by a confusing bronze sculpture of an awkwardly-proportioned horse and a tiny old man. "You interested in a tour today?"

"No, thank you. I'd just like to peruse the exhibits a bit if that's alright."

"Sure, no problem. If you like what you see, we'd appreciate it if you'd leave a small donation, or just tell your friends to come have a look."

I nodded and kept walking. I might have considered his request another time, but as it stood I had limited cash to give and no friends to invite.

I easily spent thirty minutes or more leisurely wandering the ground floor of the museum. While I'm not a great appreciator of architecture nor interior design, the manor was really rather pleasant to look at. Ornate carpets and hand-carved wood molding had obviously been fitted with great care and attention to detail. The interior had likely been refurbished in recent years, but the spirit of the original Victorian design was generally well-preserved, even if some of the museum's pieces felt strangely out of place and time.

Many of the furnishings in the parlor and the dining room, as well as the paintings on the walls, had accompanying signs detailing their histories. If these were to be believed, a large armoire and the dining set were over a century old yet still appeared to be in an impressively attractive state. The game room had no furniture, instead holding a large collection of antique vases, sculptures, wood carvings, and various other miscellaneous art. Most of the pieces appeared to be Asian in origin, but most prominent cultures from around the world were represented somewhere in the room. The sun room had an inexplicably vast array of paintings of fruit, which I only then realized where unusually abundant in other rooms as well. The sign made specific mention of this collection, but no reasons for its existence were offered. Perhaps it was not my place to question another man's obsession with fruit. I turned back and proceeded up the stairs, passing an impressive row of tall stained-glass windows and a portrait of a woman standing amid a grove of trees, which of course bore bright red apples.

The second floor's most notable feature seemed to be a large set of double doors. The sign beside the doors clearly indicated this room was off-limits without accompaniment by a tour guide. Of course, I at once became incorporeal and drifted through the locked door, into an enormous gallery. A long wooden table stood in the center of the room, lined with rows of high-backed wooden chairs. In most of these chairs, mannequins dressed in luxuriant Victorian clothing were seated and posed as though I had just floated in on them in the midst of enjoying their afternoon tea. Despite their simple plastic faces with mostly blank expressions, they had an uncanny sense of livelihood about them. This was even more pronounced when they all turned as one to look at me.

If they could see my face at that moment, as it appeared they could, they must have seen the utterly flabbergasted expression I was wearing. Their crude faces seemed to twist into similar expressions, some with a hint of fear or disgust mixed with their surprise, and perhaps a touch of anger. The round one nearest me looked the most afraid, while a tall one near the far end of the table seemed more stoic. For a long moment, we all froze in silence.

The door opened behind me. I instinctively turned back to look as a young tour guide led a small band of Asian tourists into the room. For a moment I was distracted by this girl's sudden appearance. Her excited chattering about the history of the building was of no interest to me, but as I peered through the æther at the slightly distorted image of her face, I couldn't shake the sense that she seemed familiar to me somehow. Neither she nor her charges seemed to pay any mind to the mannequins that had come to life before my eyes. As I turned back toward the table, they all seemed to be back in their original positions, their faces neutral and lifeless as before, if still a little uncanny.

I wasn't sure what to make of all this. For the rest of the afternoon I drifted lazily in the sky above the old museum-manor, pondering what was so unusual about this place, what made it feel so magnetic. I considered going back inside in human form to confront the tour guide, but decided against it. Even if I did somehow know her, based on her age, she likely didn't know me. What's more, if I did know her but couldn't recognize her, then no doubt I had forgotten her for good reason. It was generally best in my opinion not to go digging in places where one might unearth the decayed remains of the past. As is the case with museums, most of the past is generally best left to rot, with only the more attractive bits being preserved for future appreciation.

Nevertheless, this place itself was not familiar to me, nor were the uncanny figures in the gallery. I decided to linger until close to nightfall, when most of the guests had gone. As the neighborhood grew quieter and the streetlights came on, I floated back down and through the window of the second floor hallway. There, quite unconsciously, I returned to human form, my shoes coming to rest softly on the faded maroon carpet. I could feel a presence nearby, and something pulled at me. Without thinking, I began walking down the hallway, feeling myself drawn to a particular door at the end of the hall. As I drew closer, the door unlatched and swung slowly open, filling me with a growing sense of anxiety even as my body seemed relaxed and at ease.

I walked slowly through the doorway and into a small study. The smell of aging books filled the room. As I stepped inside and closed the door behind me, I saw an old woman in a mauve Victorian dress sitting behind the ornate antique desk in the corner. She greeted me kindly and offered me a seat across from her, which I took. She had blue-gray eyes that almost lit up the room, and a smile like warm molasses that seemed to flow right through my soul, melting and engulfing all of my worldly cares and concerns. I recall thinking that she reminded me of my grandmother. I then remembered that I never knew my grandmother.

It was at that point I recognized what I was

feeling. This was a mind-altering enchantment, and a fairly potent one. I fixed my eyes on her and concentrated on resisting, pushing her influence out of my mind until I was in complete control again. She continued to smile placidly at me even as her enchantment failed.

"You're a difficult young man to charm, aren't you?"

I cracked a smirk. "What can I say? I'm hard to please, as my former lovers can attest." She didn't seem amused at that, but held a polite smile.

"Well now, I believe introductions are in order. I am Madam Hortence, and this is my home. What is your name, dear?"

"My name is none of your concern, Madam, and I'm not fond of sharing it with strangers."

"I hope I haven't put you on the defensive with that charm, dear. I just wanted to ensure you wouldn't be a danger to us. We don't often entertain guests. At least, not ones who can see us for what we are."

"And what exactly are you?"

"Why, we're like you, dear. We are students of the magical arts, gifted with potential from birth, studied and mentored by the greatest minds, and practiced in the knowledge and discipline necessary to master the elements, the physical world, and even death itself."

My ears pricked up at that. Mages are rare in modern times, but immortal mages are virtually unheard of. It was a bold claim to entertain, but she did have access to mind-influencing magic I had never seen before. If she was telling the truth, this old woman's knowledge could prove very useful.

"You've thrown off the old mortal coil, then?" I tipped my hat to her. "Good for you. It must feel pretty liberating."

She shook her head, but her smile persisted. "Not entirely, I'm afraid. While we are freed from death, we find ourselves confined to our home, to protect our secret. You see, my family has lived here in peace for quite some time, but if we ever left these grounds, I fear the outside world might uncover our secret, and that peace could be destroyed."

"Yes, I imagine a lot of people would kill for such a secret. Or worse." I crossed one leg over my lap.

She nodded. "You, on the other hand, seem to have no trouble going anywhere you wish without fear of discovery by others."

"Very little trouble, anyway. If you hadn't guessed, discretion is rather important to me as well."

"I wonder if you would be kind enough to share

that spell of yours with us, dear."

I shook my head. "That's a very personal request, considering I don't even wish to share my name. What are you willing to offer me for the spell?"

"My family has existed for many centuries, and we have acquired a wealth of knowledge. Surely we have some ancient spells that would interest you."

"Or even ancient secrets."

"Ah... So in exchange, would you like me to give you the secret to eternal life?"

"No, thank you. I've already got one."

"Curious..." She held out her arms invitingly. "Well then, I would be delighted to share anything else you would like, dear."

"Alright. As it happens, I do have something in mind..."

At that moment, I heard footsteps outside. I quickly blinked out of material existence, and the old woman grew still and lifeless. The door opened, and some more tourists peeked inside to look around the study. A woman remarked on how lovely the mannequin's dress looked, and then they went on their way. Once we were alone, the two of us returned to our previous states. I sat forward in my chair and leaned on the desk.

"The Repository."

"I beg your pardon?" she asked. I couldn't read her tone, and her face still refused to change.

"I need access to the Repository. You studied at one of the old schools, right? Under the old headmasters? They must have shown you how to access it. Show me, and I'll give you my spell."

She shook her head. "I'm sorry, but I'm afraid I can't help you."

"Why not? If you graduated from a school of magic, your professors must have given access to you at some point late in your studies."

"Didn't you graduate from a school of magic, dear?"

"Of course not! Why else would I be asking?"

"Interesting."

I wasn't sure if she really didn't know or just wouldn't tell me. It didn't matter which.

"Oh, never mind." I stood up from my chair. "I shouldn't have gotten my hopes up."

"You aren't thinking of leaving now, are you?"

"Yes I am. I thought I might go someplace less disappointing."

"But dear, you know about our home, and our secret. We can't trust you not to tell someone what you saw here today."

"I'm not exactly the town gossip, Madam. Your

secret is perfectly safe with me."

"I'm afraid I can't take that chance, dear..."

I rolled my eyes. "So what, then? Now you'll have to kill me?"

"Oh, I hope that won't be necessary," she said, still smiling warmly. "There is another way. You could join our family. Become one of us, and live in eternal peace."

"Eternal peace? In this dilapidated manor, living as a decoration for obnoxious tourists to gawk at?" I scoffed. "Whatever you've been smoking, I know a man downtown who can get me something better."

"I don't think you understand, dear. After what you have seen and heard, you *cannot* leave us."

The woman sat there calmly threatening my life, but she hadn't stopped smiling the entire time we'd been talking. It was beginning to put me on edge. I stared into her eyes trying to intimidate her, but still she maintained her unrelenting Mona Lisa visage. I could feel her beady little eyes boring into my mind again, and it was all I could bear just to stand there.

"Well, I thank you for your hospitality, or what passes for hospitality in this unnerving time capsule you call a home, but I really must be going now. Have a nice eternal life."

I turned and walked toward the door. It opened, revealing the tall Victorian gentlemen from earlier standing on the other side, blocking my exit. I ignored him and kept on walking, mentally willing myself back to æthereal form. To my great surprise, I bumped into him. I stepped back and placed my hand on the nearby wall; it wouldn't go through. The spell which I normally used to become incorporeal was so second nature to me that it barely took a thought to use, yet even as I concentrated there was something stopping it from working. I was trapped in human form. I think that is the closest I've felt in a long time to genuine panic.

"As I said, dear," the woman said calmly, "you will remain here forever. I wish there were some other way, but we can't allow our secret to be threatened. I do hope you understand."

The man in the doorway moved toward me, and I backpedaled. As he entered the room, the portly gentleman entered behind him, both of them moving toward me. I bolted toward the window. I still couldn't pass through it, and it wouldn't budge when I tried to pull it open. I turned around and saw the men closing in. The old woman was still sitting there with that damned smile on her face.

"Oh, and I do want to thank you for this," she

said, holding up a scrap of paper. "It is already proving very useful."

That's when I noticed my notebook hanging half-way out of my coat pocket, the pencil dangling freely by the string. I had no recollection of pulling it out of my pocket, but I could see the frayed end of a page torn out. My eyes jumped back to the scrap of paper in her hand. In my brief mental haze under the influence of her enchantment, she must have compelled me to write down the spell. The request that I share it willingly was never necessary. Perhaps it was some sort of test, which in her estimation I must have failed. With knowledge of my spell and its name, she had all she needed not only to cast it herself, but also to stop me from using it.

The men grabbed me by the arms. In that moment, I sensed the old woman preparing to cast something terrible. I couldn't think of many offensive spells that would be of much use at that moment. My favored spell had always made for a quick and easy escape from danger. I never thought I'd be left without it. My mind cast about wildly for options. Only one seemed to jump out. It was a trick I hadn't tried in a very long time, and for good reason, but I couldn't afford to hesitate.

"Intermissuros."

As I muttered the word, the room went cold and still, a moment frozen in time. I fixed my gaze on the old woman and gave her a defiant smirk. The light appeared to leave her eyes, though her face remained the same. With my critical moment to escape secured, I returned to æthereal form, slipped from my assailants' grip, and fell backward through the window behind me. A little too quickly, in fact. As I fell toward the ground below, I tried to focus on remaining incorporeal, but the enchantment petered out before I hit the ground. I landed clumsily on the grass, scraping my knee but luckily not sustaining any serious injury. I scrambled back to my feet and took off running. I never looked back, but I could swear I felt the old woman's eyes on me the whole time.

Even in the noble heyday of magic, the average mage didn't know about Interrupts, and those who did refrained from using them without a very good reason. Everything in the universe is governed by rules, including magic. Attempting to break those rules carries a penalty. As is often the case with such things, repeat offenders face harsher penalties. I tried to tell myself I'd be fine, that my access to magic would return in short order, but I really didn't know for certain how long it would take. In the meantime, I was all alone, powerless, and totally vulnerable to any half-crazed immortals whose metaphorical tea I may have spat in that day. If I hoped to survive, I needed somewhere secure to hide away, in plain view of other people; somewhere they weren't likely to risk following me. I was going to need a plan.

Chapter 3: The Madam's Apprentice

I always had a passion for history. As a little girl, I loved to spend my free time in the library, mostly reading old novels about times long past, some classics and some recent period pieces, and maybe the odd alternate history thriller here and there. Other kids loved modern fantasy novels, high fantasy with elves and dragons, or sci-fi stories set in some far-flung future. Those were all okay, but to me, the past had an indescribable magic all its own. That's why I decided way before I started college that I would become a historian, and it's why I jumped at the chance to work with my Uncle Jim during the summer at the Lewis Building.

"Hey. How was the turnout?" he asked me as I brought the cash box back to his office.

"Not great," I said. "Just the two private tours today, and one was just two people."

"Tourism season is pretty much over. We're lucky to still be getting visitors at all, let alone on a Wednesday afternoon."

"It's just stupid." I put the box on the table next to him and crossed my arms. "People will throw away

$15 to sit in a chair and watch some stupid action movie for three hours, but they won't spend half that time and money exploring a beautiful piece of our city's history."

"You're preaching to the choir, Viv. I wish more people were as excited about old buildings as you are. Maybe I could retire early."

He glanced at his watch. Since we just closed, it was probably about 7:15. Practically every night I worked for the past two summers, we'd go through a little play-act around this time. He'd tell me I could go on home now, he just needs to sweep up a little before he leaves. I'd say I could do that for him. He'd insist, and I'd insist. He used to put up a fight, but his heart hadn't been in it lately. The fact is, he trusts me to lock up for him; he wouldn't have given me my own key otherwise. More than that, he knew that I knew he was glad to go home a little early.

"Alright," he said, getting up from his chair. "I guess I'll let you get to it. Thanks again, Viv."

"No problem," I said, giving him a quick hug. "I'll see you Friday."

"Yup." He grabbed his coat and headed out the door. "Don't stay too late."

"I won't," I called back. I stood by the desk for a bit as I listened to his footsteps fade into the distance.

Uncle Jim never questioned why I wanted to stay after closing so much. I just hoped he never would.

I spent a few minutes sweeping up around the main hall, but I was just going through the motions. There was never much dust to worry about anyway. I think Madam Hortence takes care of that somehow. She's so wonderful, I thought. She's done more to preserve this beautiful place than anybody. I'm so lucky to have met her.

After putting the broom away, I headed upstairs toward the gallery. I knocked lightly on the door and slowly opened it. Inside, everyone had already assembled around the table. Madam Hortence sat at the head of the table as usual. Even from across the room, I felt surrounded by the warmth of her loving, enigmatic smile.

"Vivian, dear," she said. "You're just in time. Please, have a seat."

"Yes, Madam." I curtsied to the ladies and gentlemen, and joined them at the table.

"I don't believe you've heard about the bit of trouble we had yesterday." She paused to drink from the teacup in front of her.

I frowned. "Trouble?"

"A man entered our home and discovered us," said Sir Calvin, a tall slender man with wire-rimmed glasses. "In this very room, he saw us for what we truly are."

"How is that possible?" I asked, wide-eyed.

"You would not have seen him. He used magic to slip into our midst, and our illusions were not potent enough to deceive him."

"You're saying this man is a mage like you?"

"Not like us, dear," Madam Hortence clarified. "You see, magic is an exquisite art, which all of us have studied for a great many years and trained extensively to use. After meeting this man, I learned that he did not study in any school of magic. He is an adept; unrefined, undisciplined, and bearing no respect for the magical arts or those who practice them."

"His boorish attitude did nothing to redeem him either," added Sir Calvin.

"Nevertheless, I received him cordially and offered him the opportunity to join our family. He refused, and threatened to reveal us to the mortal world as he left."

"Of course, Sir Calvin and I stepped in to prevent his escape," said Mister Harold, a large man who wore a top hat. "But alas, our efforts were in vain. I fear he may be more powerful than we-"

Madam Hortence raised her hand and he

stopped. "What Mister Harold means to say is that this man took us all by surprise. He appears to be highly skilled."

Mister Harold cleared his throat. "Yes. After his escape, we were met with difficulty divining his whereabouts. I'm certain our combined efforts will locate him soon, but every moment he is out in the world puts our family at risk."

The rest of the ladies and gentlemen echoed their fears with solemn nods and murmurs of agreement.

"And so," Sir Calvin continued, "our home lies in peril, for this man may yet reveal our secret, exposing us to the cruelty and chaos of the world beyond these walls."

"That's terrible!" I stood up from my chair. "Madam Hortence, you can't let this happen!"

"Please don't be rude, dear. Sit down," she said, and took a sip from her cup.

"But..." I sat just on the edge of the chair. "If everyone finds out the truth about you all, you know what they'll do. Just look at all the old legends, the Fountain of Youth, the Holy Grail; even just a rumor of the kind of power you all have drives people to do crazy things. There's no telling what will happen to all of you, or to this place. We can't let it happen."

Madam Hortence took another long sip from her cup and set it down. "If only all mortals had hearts as pure as yours, Vivian, we could welcome them all without fear. But do not despair. There is still time to stop this fiendish man who has threatened our home, and I believe that you are the one who shall do so."

I blinked. "Me?"

Sir Calvin grinned, but said nothing.

"Madam, are you sure about this?" Mister Harold protested. "She's only a mortal girl, after all."

"We may attempt to pursue him ourselves," she said, "traveling unseen through the æther as he does, but he is far more experienced in that realm than we are. He will likely sense our approach and may escape again. On the other hand, surely he will not expect to be pursued by a mortal girl lacking any magical potential."

"And what should she do when she encounters him? If he continues to move through the æther, she may as well hope to grasp the wind in her palm. Worse, if he thinks her a nuisance-"

"I will prepare enchanted items to aid her. Once he has been found, all she must do is subdue him long enough for you and the others to come and collect him." She turned her smile toward me. "What do you say to this, Vivian? Will you accept this task I have given you, to protect our family and our home?"

I was smiling ear-to-ear before she even finished asking. "Are you kidding? Yes, of course I will! I can't wait to kick that adept guy's ass."

Madam chuckled. "I am grateful for your enthusiasm, dear, but mind your manners. Now then, if there are no further objections..."

She looked around the table, and no one said anything. Mister Harold still looked uneasy but stayed quiet.

"Very well, it is decided. Vivian, you are excused for now. Sir Calvin will begin his own pursuit of the adept immediately. However, I will require time to prepare the items for your task. Please come and meet me in my study on Friday night, half past eight o'clock, and I shall instruct you on how to proceed."

"Okay." I stood up and gave the room a quick curtsy. "Thank you so much, Madam Hortence. I promise, I won't let you down."

"I trust you won't, dear."

I turned and walked back out the door, closing it slowly as I left. Old doors like those need a gentle touch. As I started to walk back down the hall, I couldn't help but hear some of the discussion that went on after I left the room.

"Your concern is justified, Mister Harold," Sir

Calvin said, "but would you please make some effort to conceal your fear of the adept while the girl is present?"

"Did you not see what transpired? Our spells failed outright. He did not counter them; it was as though they were never cast at all. And that incantation he used: *intermissuros,* was it? Can any one of you hope to glean what that spell is or how it works? I'm not even certain it *is* a spell."

I kept walking. I didn't need to hear any more. In a moment, Madam Hortence would defend me and reassure Mister Harold. She knew what she was doing. After all, she never would have asked me to go after this guy if she didn't know for certain I could handle it. It might be a little dangerous, but there was probably nothing to worry about. Madam Hortence is so caring, and she has always put her trust in me.

I thought back to almost a year ago, when she first introduced me to her family and told me about their life here, Mister Harold was losing it. But Madam Hortence saw something in me that she liked, and Sir Calvin said he saw it too. I remember after I left that night, I overheard Mister Harold still worrying about putting their trust in me, and Madam Hortence let him know he had nothing to worry about. When he asked how she could be so sure, she just said in her sweet voice, "Because she is kind and innocent, and pure of heart. She will be easy to control."

...Wait, no, that doesn't seem right. I must have remembered it wrong.

I was never really the superstitious type, but it was hard to explain what I had seen that day on the stairs. Until then I never thought I might literally be chasing a ghost. Afterward, I had to seriously consider the possibility. In any case, whoever or whatever this guy was, I had no intention of letting him get away from me again.

Whenever I had any spare time around the station, I kept compiling files on crimes I attributed to my ghost. As incredible as it all seemed, the pattern was undeniable to me. I even got up the nerve to email some of my findings to the chief, and told him my theory that this guy was a career criminal who had probably been eluding the police for years. The chief didn't completely write me off, but he didn't sound convinced either. He agreed to send word for officers to keep an eye out for the guy, but that was it. As it turns out, that's all I needed.

About a week went by before I got a message from a nearby precinct. Officers downtown had to deal with a public disturbance call, a bunch of homeless guys getting rowdy and drunk in the park. They arrested two men who seemed to be instigating and harassing the officers who responded. One of them perfectly matched the description of my suspect, right down to his clothes. I got on the phone with them and asked to come by and talk to him. They agreed.

That Wednesday evening I was sitting in an interrogation room in the neighboring police station. An officer brought in the ghost and sat him in a chair at the table across from where I sat.

"He's all yours. Have fun."

The way he said it, the officer could have been directing the comment at either one of us. He walked back out and closed the door, leaving us alone.

For a few long seconds, I just stared at the man, studying him. I could definitely see why the arresting officers took him for a homeless guy. He was in much rougher shape than the last time we met. His clothes were dirty and wrinkled, his hat was smudged with dirt around the brim. He had dark circles under his eyes, and just the hint of a beard suggesting he hadn't shaved in a day or two. He stared down at the table, his expression blank.

"Having a rough day?" I asked.

"To put it mildly."

He didn't look up from the table, but yawned exaggeratedly.

Something didn't add up. With all the time I'd

spent looking for any trace of this guy, I thought he had to be some kind of master criminal. And yet, here he was sitting in front of me in handcuffs, after being picked up off the side of the road by a squad car responding to a public disturbance. The way they described it, it's like he wanted to be caught.

"So," I said, "they tell me you haven't called anyone since you've been here. You don't have anyone you want to call at a time like this?"

"No," he said calmly. He almost sounded bored.

"No family, friends...?"

"None left. I much prefer solitude anyway."

"Well then, you could at least talk to a lawyer. God knows you'll need a good one."

"Oh, I really doubt that," he said, leaning back in his chair.

"Is that so?"

I opened my briefcase and dramatically dropped my folder full of case files on the table. They were all tough to pin on him, but he didn't know that, and I thought the sheer number of them was pretty intimidating. He just scoffed and rolled his eyes.

"I have quite a few questions I'd like to ask you about the cases in this folder before they get passed on to the DA, but for now let's start with this one: who are you?"

He smirked. "Who would you like me to be, Detective? Whatever name or persona you're chasing, I'm sure I can accommodate you for the moment. Otherwise, I suppose I am no one."

I sighed and leaned in close. "Listen, I don't know how you've kept dodging the police for so long, but whatever tricks you've got up your sleeve, they're not going to help you anymore. It's over; I've got enough evidence here to put you away for a very long time. Multiple counts of burglary, petty theft, possible breaking and entering, and that's just to name a few."

He slowly shook his head, still smirking. "Evidence is a funny thing. People are more inclined to believe what they wish than to believe what their eyes show them. Especially if what their eyes show them is beyond their comprehension."

I eased back into my chair a bit. He seemed like he was just toying with me, and he obviously wasn't intimidated. I had to find a way to probe deeper.

"They tell me you didn't eat your dinner, either," I said, crossing my arms.

"Is that what that was? I wasn't sure what that tray of slop was meant to be. It certainly didn't resemble food."

"Well, it's as good as you're going to get in jail, so you'd better get used to it."

"No, I don't think so. I'd just as soon not eat. Perhaps I'll find something more palatable after I leave here."

"That could be quite a long wait. You know, they haven't even finished processing you yet. Once these charges are filed, you'll still be here a while until a judge can see you to set bail. And from the sound of it, you don't really have anyone to come and post bail for you anyway, so you're really looking at a long stay."

"By my reckoning of time, I give it another day or two at most. After that, I'll be on my way."

That irked me a bit, but I hid it with a smile.

"Really?"

He nodded.

"And just how do you plan on leaving, huh? You know, this isn't some corner store or a run-down apartment building with a broken buzzer. You can't take five steps outside this room without running into a cop or getting caught on surveillance cameras. A man in your position can't just get up and walk out of here."

He hummed quietly to himself. "You're right, I suppose. Though walking wasn't really what I had in mind..."

I stopped smiling. There was something really

off about this guy. He was too sure of himself. Maybe he could tell I was new at this and wasn't taking me seriously, but it felt like more than that. He kept glancing at my face like he was expecting to see something different.

"Shall we dispense with the charade, Detective?" he asked. "You're not really here about some petty theft charges or an intoxicated brouhaha in the park, are you? What is it you really want from me? Because whatever it is, I don't think I can help you."

I wasn't sure what to make of that. I was there for a legitimate investigation, but maybe my interest did run a little deeper than I was willing to admit. In any case, I wasn't about to have the interrogation turned around on me, and he was clearly giving me nothing for now. As for his alleged escape, I didn't know what he was planning, but I figured whatever it was, the police department could handle it.

"Alright," I said, gathering up my files. "I've got some other work to do. We'll continue this another time."

He shrugged. "If you say so."

I stood up and walked to the door. The guard opened it and I stepped out of the room. "I'm done with him," I said, then turned and walked away. I still had stacks of paperwork waiting at my desk. I could deal with the wannabe master criminal later. After all, I thought, it wasn't like he'd be going anywhere anytime soon.

I finished up my day's work and returned to the station where the ghost was being held later that night. The place was pretty empty, except for the handful of guards placed near the doors, and the one guy watching over the few people in their cells. I showed him my badge and he gave me a go-ahead wave, barely looking at it. I figured he must have been on duty for a while, because he seemed like he had a hard time keeping his eyes open.

"You might want to grab a coffee," I remarked to him.

He muttered something unintelligible back to me.

I continued past him, looking into the cells until I found the ghost. He was sitting on the cot facing the wall, looking bored with the world. I tapped on the glass pane in the middle of the door, and he looked up at me. I flashed him the same cocky smirk he'd shown me earlier. He responded by casually flipping me the bird.

"Could you come open this cell, please?" I looked to where the guard was sitting, but he didn't respond. "Hello?"

I walked back to find him fast asleep, still sitting upright in his chair. I chuckled a bit and gently shook him by the shoulder. He didn't respond. I shook him a little harder and yelled in his ear a bit. I banged on the table in front of him. Still nothing. He just sat there, chest slowly rising and falling.

As I watched the guard, apparently deep in the most restful sleep of his life, I began to realize how quiet the whole station was. I walked back down the hall a bit and looked into all the cells. There were only two other people being held there that night. Both of them were lying on their cots, fast asleep. I looked up at a clock on the wall; 8:59 PM. I started to think my guy was somehow behind this, but that didn't make sense. Even if he could have done it, why would he knock the guys in the other cells out?

Then I started to feel it again. That weird, paranoid feeling. I'd felt it a little the last few times I saw the ghost, but it was much worse now. The feeling I got from him was kind of like a low throbbing headache, but this one was like a sharp searing knife into my brain. I could almost taste it; the sensation seemed to fill the air around me, and waves of it were flowing over me, all coming from the same direction. It wasn't coming from the direction of his cell. It was coming from behind me, back toward the entrance where I'd come in. I could feel a knot forming in my stomach. I swallowed hard, took a slow deep breath, and turned around.

Two figures were coming down the hall. I couldn't actually see them, but somehow I could feel their presence. In my mind, I got the impression of shadows sliding across the floor, as if cast by a hanging lamp slowly swinging from the ceiling. At least that's how they moved. I couldn't make out any more details. They seemed to disappear completely if I looked directly at them, but as I turned my eyes away a bit, I could just make out their shapes. They were slowly drawing closer to me. I thought of my gun, then realized it probably wouldn't do me any good. As they kept drawing closer, I took a deep breath and stood my ground, waiting to see what they'd do.

To my surprise, they kept on moving slowly past me. Or through me. I'm not really sure which. I was standing right there in their path, but I never felt them touch me. *That's it*, I thought, *I'm definitely going crazy*. I turned and watched as they kept moving down the hall. They got to my suspect's cell, turned and drifted inside as if the door wasn't even there. I could hear him jump to his feet. His voice was muffled, but I could just barely make out his words.

"You'd really come this far from home? You're bolder than I thought." Suddenly, there was a loud bang against the door of the cell, and I heard him shouting into the hall. "Detective! If you have any clever plans to keep me here, now would be the time to employ them!"

Moments later, the shadows reemerged from the cell, now with another shadow floating between them. They were drifting back down the hall in unison while the middle one seemed to be struggling against them. It was him, I was sure of it. I watched their movement, my mind racing.

As the shadows drew closer, my instincts suddenly took over, and I ran straight toward them. Focusing on the struggling shadow, I reached out my hands and grasped at nothing. Instead of empty air, my fingers found the fabric of his coat. I grabbed hold of the coat tightly and pulled back hard, stumbling awkwardly as he suddenly emerged from nowhere and fell right on top of me. I must have looked almost as shocked as he did. The shadows circled around us as we both scrambled to our feet.

"How did you do that?" the ghost demanded. "You can manipulate æther?"

"I don't know what the hell you're talking about. What are these things?" I gestured to the shadows. They had us surrounded, blocking the hallway in both directions, but hesitated to get any closer to us once we were both standing. I wasn't sure if it was me or him that gave them pause now.

The ghost gave me a puzzled look, blinked, then chuckled to himself. "Wow. So much potential going to waste... Still, this is quite a development. You're not at all what I was expecting, Detective."

"That goes for you, too." I warily looked around at the ominous shadowy forms. "Look, whoever you are, maybe we can help each other here. For a start, how about you just tell me what the hell is going on?"

"You're a bright man. You can find your own answers." He looked down at his hand, slowly waved his fingers about, and smiled. "Fortunately, it seems my time is up. I'll be taking my leave now."

"You've got to be kidding me."

The shadows still had the hallway blocked in either direction, but that didn't seem to concern him. He turned to me and smirked as he pulled the brim of his hat down a bit.

"It was Detective Powers, right? I think I'll remember you."

With that, he turned and ran right into a solid

wall, as if it weren't even there. Instantly, his body seemed to evaporate and completely vanished through the wall, air whooshing gently around to fill the empty space where he'd been. The shadows turned and lurched after him, sliding through the same wall, and disappeared. The air suddenly felt a lot clearer as they left.

I stood and stared at the wall in disbelief. Gingerly, I stepped forward and placed my hand on the wall. It was solid brick, at least a few feet thick. I took a deep breath and tried to calmly convince myself that I was not going crazy.

I wasn't convinced.

Chapter 5: Paranormal Crimes

The chief in my precinct is in his late fifties, completely gray-haired including his mustache, and while I'd only met him the one time before, his stony expression and serious demeanor left a strong impression. He's just under six feet tall, but he's an imposing figure even to larger men. I was nervous as hell that first time I met him. He had told me he knows people, and he could tell I had potential. He might have meant it to be encouraging, but it mostly sounded like I had high expectations to live up to if I wanted to keep my job.

The other precinct was apparently blaming me for the disappearance of an unidentified homeless man from his holding cell, so the next morning when I heard the chief wanted to speak privately with me at his desk, I was expecting the absolute worst.

"Before I start, do you have anything you want to say for yourself?" he asked.

His voice was just as deep and gravely as I remembered. I shifted in my seat and cleared my throat.

"Sir, I swear I never removed the suspect from his cell. He escaped by... some other means. I'm sorry,

I can't really explain what happened last night."

"Then maybe we should have a look together. I asked for the video surveillance footage to be sent over here."

He turned the computer monitor on his desk so I could see it from where I sat. On the screen were grainy black-and-white images of the night before. One shot showed the guard half-asleep in his chair. Another showed the hallway lined with holding cells. The chief pressed a key on his keyboard, and the video began playing.

I saw myself walking up to the guard, over to the cell, and back to the guard to find him asleep. The image of me started looking around in horrified confusion, apparently at nothing at all, then abruptly ran half-way down the hall. For a moment, I thought this was solid proof I was losing my mind. Then, just as I remembered, the ghost appeared out of thin air and fell on top of me. We both got up and talked for a moment, and he turned and ran right through a solid wall. There was no evidence of any shadow creatures, but the rest was all there. My jaw dropped a bit, and to my even greater surprise, the chief cracked a smile.

"So," he said, "I guess your instincts were right about this one..." He thoughtfully stroked his mustache. "Well, you at least talked to him before he escaped. Did you find out anything about him, where he came from, maybe a name?"

He seemed to be taking this supernatural revelation a lot better than I was. I needed a second to find the words to respond.

"Uh... No, not really. Just that he seemed confident he was going to escape." I took a breath and tried to steady my nerves. There was no point in holding anything back at this point. "It seems like he has some enemies that are... like him. I was seeing something or someone there trying to break him out, but they aren't showing up on the video. Whatever they were, he didn't want to go with them. I don't really know what's going on, only that whatever it is, we've barely scratched the surface."

"That's what I was afraid of. I guess there's no avoiding this any longer."

The chief turned the monitor back to its normal position, then slowly pushed his chair back. He opened the top drawer on his desk and reached inside. For some reason, he'd closed his eyes and was searching through the drawer by touch.

"Powers, have you ever heard of something called the Paranormal Crimes Provision?"

"No sir, I haven't."

"I wouldn't think so. Most people don't take it

seriously anyway, but as it turns out, there are around a dozen cities across the country with dedicated units in charge of investigating crimes that are 'paranormal' in nature, though they're never advertised as such. They don't handle too many cases, but the ones they do are usually pretty extraordinary, and always well hidden from the press. Our jurisdiction does not have an active paranormal crimes unit. However, after I reviewed that footage this morning, I thought it would be in everyone's best interest to establish one."

He opened his eyes. From the drawer, he pulled out a small booklet and slid it across the desk to me. It looked like a section of the county penal code, but I didn't recognize the heading or section number.

"What is this?" I asked.

"Your new job description. As of today, I'm putting you in charge of the newly-formed Special Investigative Unit for this precinct. But before we make it official, I need to know I can trust you not to make me look foolish for doing this. We can't have word getting out about our detectives chasing after ghosts and goblins. We'd be a complete laughing stock, whether they're real or not. Your duty is to handle these matters by-the-books, and with all possible discretion. Is that clear?"

"Uh... Yes, sir."

"Good. Believe me, I don't take this whole thing lightly. Unfortunately, we are still short on man-power around here, and the people we do have available I wouldn't want to trust with a secret like this. So for now your unit won't be much of a unit. I'll see about getting you an intern to help with the office work, but for the most part you'll be on your own. Think you can handle it?"

"Yes sir. I'll, uh, do my best."

The whole thing felt too bizarre to be real, but I didn't want to be the one to tell the chief he sounded as crazy as I was. Better to just go with it.

"Your first case is to investigate this ghost of ours. Find out everything you can about him, and I mean everything: who he is, where he came from, where he lives, where he spends his time, who he associates with, and especially how to catch him for more than a day. And remember, all of this has to stay between us. Understood?"

"Absolutely," I said, nodding excitedly. "I won't let you down, sir."

"Alright. Now go on, get to it."

"Yes sir. Thank you."

I took the booklet and hurried out of the room, eager to dive head-first into the investigation. I still wasn't totally sure that the chief and I hadn't both lost our minds. Maybe this was all just a dream. Maybe it was some big elaborate joke at my expense. All I knew for sure was that chasing ghosts hadn't lost me my job yet, so for the time being I was going to seize this opportunity. Sooner or later this guy was going to slip up and get caught again, and with any luck I was going to be the one to catch him.

My big promotion took effect the same day. I was officially the lead detective for the newly-formed Special Investigative Unit, which kind of sounds impressive if you ignore the fact that there's only one detective in the unit. The job wasn't exactly glamorous either. With my suspect currently in the wind, I was back to digging through police reports for possible clues.

By late afternoon the space on my desk was once again being dominated by tall stacks of reports, though at this point it was mostly older files. I had to appreciate the irony. I spent years working hard to get a promotion and get out from behind my desk, and instead I stacked more paperwork on top of it. At least this way I got to focus on the reports that caught my interest the most, looking for things out of place that could point to the ghost.

I had also hung up a city map on the cork board

on the wall by my desk to better track the ghost's activity. I was just sliding a new pin into the map when I heard my name.

"John?"

When I turned around I was greeted by the cheery face of one of the older ladies from the human resources office. I silently hoped the fact that her name escaped me would not come up. She was followed by a young guy I didn't recognize, probably in his late teens or early twenties.

"My goodness, just look at all this." She gestured to my desk. "Must be some big case you're working on. I hope I'm not interrupting."

I wasn't sure how sincere she was being; there might have been a hint of condescension in her voice. If general murmurs around the department were to be believed, most people were not under the impression I was moving up in the world.

"No, it's no problem," I said.

"John, this is James Klein. He's a criminal justice student going into his junior year at city college. He's just started his summer internship with us today."

"Nice to meet you, James." I offered a handshake, which he enthusiastically accepted.

"You too, Detective Powers."

For a smaller guy, he had a surprisingly strong grip, made more noticeable by the fact that he kept the handshake going a bit longer than it should have lasted.

"This is such an amazing opportunity for me," he continued. "I've wanted to become a detective ever since I was a kid. I've read about all the greats. Of course I'm also studying forensic science this year and I'd totally love to be part of a CSI team. But right now I'll take any experience I can get. This is actually my first time inside a police station. This is so cool. I'm really excited to be here."

"I noticed."

"Sorry, am I talking too much? I do that when I get excited. Anyway, I'm really looking forward to working with you, Detective Powers."

"You're going to be interning with *me*? Wow, that was fast."

"He was actually supposed to be shadowing Detective Smith today," the lady interjected. "But there was a bit of a... personality conflict. Anyway, I spoke with the chief and he recommended placing James with you."

"Well, I'd certainly appreciate the help. There's a lot to go through here."

"Perfect. Sounds like you're both eager to get

started, so I won't hold you up any longer. Stay out of trouble now, you two."

She giggled and walked away, taking any concern I had about remembering her name along with her. James looked at me and smiled.

"It's really an honor to be working with you. I heard people saying you're like some kind of prodigy."

I furrowed my brow. "Are you sure they were talking about me?"

"Yeah. Somebody in the HR office was saying when you got out of high school you got a full-ride scholarship to city college. He sounded pretty jealous, actually."

"Oh..." My eyes started wandering instinctively toward the floor, but I pulled them back up to meet his. "I think I know who that was. No, it's nothing like that. The Brighter Futures scholarship is a need-based award. I mean, grades are a factor, but I wasn't top of my class or anything." His smile faded as I went on. "And anyway, the city schools don't really have the best reputation around here. To some people, it's just a step above taking night classes at community college. Of course there's nothing wrong with that route either, but there are always people who will look down on you for it. Between that, my age, and the fact that I didn't put in my time on the street, there are more than a few people who feel like I haven't really earned my place here."

"Damn." James shook his head. "Those bastards. I didn't really get it at the time, but they were totally making fun of you behind your back. How are you not more mad about this right now?"

I shrugged. "It's fine."

"It's not fine! You shouldn't let people push you around like that. Why don't you go down there and give them hell?"

"I'm still the new guy here. I don't want to risk my job by starting something with somebody. Maybe I could say something in a few years if they're still giving me trouble. I get the feeling some of the old guys don't respect me for more than just my lack of experience..." I cracked a smile. "You know what, though? The beauty of it is, it really doesn't matter what they think. I know I've been doing my best here, and the chief has obviously seen that too. He had enough trust in me to promote me and let me work on the case I wanted. I've got the opportunity of a lifetime here, and I'm taking advantage of it. Maybe I'm not going to be the most popular guy around the department. But the fact is, as cliched as this might sound, I'm not here to make friends. I'm here to do a job, to see that justice is served."

James' eyes had gotten significantly wider as I spoke. Standing there staring at me, he kind of looked like a kid meeting his favorite superhero. I shifted my feet awkwardly. He smiled and grabbed my hand to give it another vigorous shake.

"I'll say it again: it's an honor to be working with you, boss."

"Thanks, James."

He nodded, then looked over the contents of my desk. "So, what are we working on here?"

"We're working on finding this guy." I picked up the sketch of the ghost I'd had made earlier that day and handed it to James. "He's about the most successful and elusive career criminal you've never heard of. I still don't even know his name yet. I'm trying to establish a pattern of his activity to get some clue about where he might pop up next."

I gestured to the stacks of reports that were threatening to fall off my desk if they got much taller.

"These are all reports from unsolved crimes, some going back ten years. Most of them are dead ends, but more than a few of these are bound to be his handiwork. This is where you come in. I need help going through these to find any trace of my suspect. If you see any really bizarre circumstances, especially eyewitness accounts describing somebody who looks like that sketch, show it to me and I'll decide if it should go on the map."

"How do you decide if a crime might be him?"

"I've been tracking this guy for a little while now. I'm starting to get a sense for how he operates. It's a little hard to explain, but when I see a case with seemingly nothing to go on, sometimes I can just tell it's his work. Plus, that hat of his usually gives him away if there are any witnesses"

"Okay..." He took a report from the stack and started reading through it. "So, what exactly has this guy done to get your attention? Or what do you think he's done?"

I figured this would have to come up soon enough. The report he was looking at was on a theft at a convenience store. These weren't the kinds of crimes you would expect detectives to dedicate a lot of time to. I gave him an apologetic look.

"Sorry, I can't really discuss that. Some of the specifics of this case are kind of sensitive in nature."

"Ah." James gave me a knowing nod in return. "Got it. Say no more, boss."

I smiled, relieved he let the subject drop so easily. I'm not a great liar, and I wouldn't want to start a professional relationship with a lie anyway. The chief was pretty clear about need-to-know with this case:

the only people who needed to know were me and him. Hopefully James' enthusiasm to learn about detective work didn't come with too much curiosity.

He pulled up a chair beside me, and the two of us got down to business.

I returned to the Lewis Building on Friday night and went to my uncle's office to wait. I sat in his chair and eyed the clock on the wall, tapping my foot on the floor. I assumed Madam Hortence had good reason for wanting me to wait until 8:30, so I did my best to contain my excitement. As time stretched on, I started to think about what the man I was supposed to find would be like, how he'd look, how he'd react to me finding him. Maybe he would attack me when he realized who sent me, or else just run away. I wondered if he would just talk to me if I approached carefully. I'm five-foot-three, five-fourish in my black leather boots, and about a hundred and ten pounds soaking wet. I'm not exactly a threatening figure, no matter how stompy and bad-ass my boots are.

Then again, he might just ignore me. Maybe I'm no threat to him no matter who sent me. After all, I'm just a normal human, and he's an experienced magic user. Madam Hortence had called him an "adept", which sounds pretty scary when you think about its meaning; basically all the incredible power of a mage with none of the discipline.

I kept watching the clock until it read 8:30, then

jumped to my feet and practically ran upstairs to the study. I could just about hear my heart pounding in my ears from the anticipation. I knocked lightly on the door.

"Come in," Madam Hortence's gentle voice answered from inside.

I opened the door and was met by her warm, inviting smile. I stepped inside, and she walked up to meet me, carrying a small jewelry box.

"Sir Calvin was able to locate the adept," she said, "but as I feared, we were not able to capture him. He knows now that we are pursuing him. It is even more important that you find him and stop him quickly. As promised, I have some items to help you on your way, Vivian."

She set the box on the desk and opened it. From inside she picked up a thin gold necklace, and gestured for me to lean forward so she could place it around my neck. A small compass hung from the center of it.

"This will help me find him?" I guessed.

"It will, and then some. When you feel you are getting closer to your goal, give the necklace a light squeeze. That will activate a spell which will allow you to see into the æther. He will have nowhere to hide from you. Grasp the necklace again when you no longer have need of the enchantment."

"Thank you, Madam."

"Also, take this."

She took my right hand and slid a large ornate ring onto my finger. The brilliant blue sapphire seemed to light up the room.

"It's beautiful. What does it do?"

"I have imbued it with a magic bolt spell which should subdue anyone it strikes without otherwise harming them. To use it, simply point the stone toward your target, and press your thumb against the band to activate it. One bolt will likely be enough, but the enchantment should allow for as many bolts as you need."

I must have had the biggest, silliest grin on my face at that moment, but who could blame me? Not many girls get to shoot magic lightning out of their hands.

"I believe you are ready, dear. I wish I could prepare you further, but it is difficult to know what to expect from this one. However, if you remain calm and keep your wits about you, I'm certain you will be just fine."

"Again, thank you, Madam." I gave her a polite curtsy. "I'll do my best."

"I know you will, dear."

With that, she sent me on my way.

I spent the next couple of hours changing buses and walking the streets of the city, following the needle on my compass. Every now and then, the needle seemed to go a little crazy, whirling around like it couldn't tell where to point, but eventually it would settle on a direction and I'd continue the hunt. This happened more and more as I went along. I knew I was getting closer.

The compass was leading me downtown, farther than I'd ever gone before. My parents would probably be upset to find out I was walking around a neighborhood like this by myself in the middle of the night, but I knew I'd be fine. If the pepper spray in my pocket wasn't enough to keep me safe, the lightning bolt ring would be.

Finally, I found myself standing outside a large dilapidated brick building. The paint on the faded sign over the door had mostly peeled off; it was impossible to read anymore. The compass needle was spinning continuously and wouldn't stop.

"This must be the place," I muttered to myself.

I squeezed the necklace between my fingers, and suddenly the sign became even more faded. Then the whole building was. I watched in awe as everything around me seemed to change. Colors were becoming muted and grayish, and the edges all seemed to flow into each other like some impressionist oil painting. I looked down at the sidewalk and tapped on it with my foot. I watched the concrete melt and flow under me like a river of molasses, even as I felt and heard it solidly connect with my shoe.

"Freaky."

I looked up at the building again. This time I could see something else, like a dull light shining through the flowing walls far above. I carefully made my way up the steps and opened the front door. It looked like the lobby of an old hotel I read about once, though it was a bit hard to tell with all the shapes flowing and blending into each other. I made my way to the stairwell and began slowly climbing the steps toward the eerie light. I tried my best not to make noise, but each and every step let out an awful creak when I stepped on it.

As I kept ascending, the light grew brighter. I reached the floor it was coming from and started sneaking down the hall. My target was definitely in the room to my right. I stopped in front of the door and just stood there for a few moments. Through the flowing gray paint of the door, I could just make out the source of the light, a human shape apparently hovering close to the ceiling of the room. I couldn't be sure, but it seemed like it was looking right back at me.

Okay, don't panic, I thought. How should I approach this?

My mind had been racing on the way here, imagining all sorts of plans and scenarios for how I could handle this guy. I couldn't think of a single one in that moment. So instead, I decided to improvise. I knocked on the door, and shouted in my cheeriest voice:

"Housekeeping!"

The human figure inside suddenly dropped to the floor and the light faded. I grabbed my necklace, and my vision slowly returned to normal. I took a breath to steady my nerves, then tried the handle. When I found it was unlocked, I slowly opened the door.

The room inside was barren aside from an old mattress, which still looked newer than the rest of the building, and a few paper grocery bags sitting in the corner. A man in his mid-thirties sat cross-legged on the mattress, wearing a faded white dress shirt, brown vest, and matching brown slacks and loafers. The outfit looked like he could have stolen it straight from my grandfather's closet. The one mismatched part was the black bowler hat on his head.

"Well it's about time," he said with a smirk. "The service here is utterly horrendous. There haven't been fresh linens on this bed in at least half a century. And don't get me started on the bathroom."

I clenched my fist at my side, feeling the ring on my finger. He didn't seem all that threatening, but something about this guy made me really nervous.

"Who are you?" I asked.

"You don't know? Then why have you been following me?"

I swallowed. I didn't know what to say anymore. If he found out the truth, there was no telling what he'd do. He slowly looked me up and down, and his eyes lingered on my necklace. At least, that's what I hoped he was staring at.

"You seem like a nice girl," he said finally. "What are you doing in this part of town, playing with magical toys, chasing someone you don't know anything about? You don't have anything better to do on a Friday night?"

"You threatened somebody I care about," I said finally. "I won't let you endanger them."

He chuckled. "You won't let me?"

He stood up off the bed and took a step toward me, still looking me over, grinning slightly. I'd never felt so small in my life as I did at that moment. The fact that he was a good half a foot taller than me didn't help.

"Just who are you trying to protect anyway? The detective? You seem a little young for him. Not that I'm one to talk."

I didn't know who he was talking about, and he saw it in my expression.

"No? Then... don't tell me..." The grin faded from his face. "That old bitch."

Feeling a sudden rush of anger, I held up my fist and pointed the ring toward him.

"You take that back," I said as firmly as I could. "Madam Hortence is a kind and wonderful lady, and she deserves your respect. She's never done anything to you. All she cares about is protecting her family and living in peace. I don't care who or what you are; I won't let you do anything to hurt her."

"You sad, deluded little creature. She's really set up camp inside your head, hasn't she?"

"I'm not afraid of you," I lied. The words were flowing out of me more or less on their own. "I know what you are. You're an adept, just a wannabe-mage who plays with magic but doesn't respect or understand its principles. You threatened to reveal Madam Hortence and her sanctuary to the world. I won't let that happen."

"You really have no idea, do you?" He clicked his tongue. "Poor thing. It might be funny if it weren't so pathetic."

I pressed my finger against the ring. A bolt of light lit up the whole room as it leaped out of the ring, straight toward where he was standing, but not fast enough. As soon as I'd touched the band, he disappeared leaving only a faint cloud of dust behind. The bolt shot straight through the far wall, but didn't even damage the peeling wallpaper as it dispersed.

"Think about it: why would I possibly care about her precious little retirement home?"

I instinctively spun around to look for him, but his voice seemed to come from inside my own head.

"I never threatened them. I'll wager that loony old bird is just annoyed that there's someone in town with more power than she has."

"You're lying."

I grabbed my necklace, and the world shifted back to the wispy gray of the æther. I looked up and saw him floating just over my head, surrounded in the same pale aura I'd seen before. I pointed my hand up and fired another bolt. This time I saw him move, but just barely. He'd glided halfway across the room before the bolt had even left the ring.

"And she told you I was an adept?" He chuckled. *"I can't tell whether she's going senile, or she's just filling your pretty little head with lies."*

I clenched my teeth and shot another bolt at him. Again, he dodged it easily, gliding through the wall and into the hallway. I stomped out through the doorway and glared at him as he floated there.

"Listen you creep: Madam Hortence is a wonderful lady! She's smart and kind, and she'd never lie to me. She's a great mage, too. There's no way she'd ever be jealous of someone like you. In fact, I think you're the one who's jealous of her."

He laughed again. *"You know, I was almost considering breaking that nasty little curse she has on you, but I think you might be more fun this way."*

I shot at him once again. This time he zoomed straight up through the ceiling. I looked up and watched the light from his aura fade from sight.

"Come back, you coward!" I shouted after him.

Not a second later, I felt a hand on my neck. As I whirled around to face him, he ripped the necklace away from me. I jumped back as my vision snapped back to normal, and I was hit with a sudden wave of vertigo. I stumbled and leaned on the wall to keep from falling.

"Those seeing spells never did have very long

range to them," he said.

I scowled and stared up at him as he inspected the compass.

"And this is the location spell they keep bombarding me with, huh? Good to know."

He shoved the necklace in his pocket, and I pointed the ring at him.

"You give that back," I said, trying and failing to sound tough.

He smirked. "Scared little girls shouldn't play with magic items. You might hurt yourself."

"Piss off, creeper!"

I shot at him again. He disappeared, and now I couldn't see where to. He had the upper hand and he knew it. I had to try to turn things in my advantage.

"You're calling me scared? You seem like you're the one running scared. Why not stand and fight me?"

"That would be no fight at all." His voice came from behind me, and I whipped around to face him. "And unlike some unsavory sorts, I have no interest in abusing young girls. I'm giving you a chance to come to your senses and flee before things become unpleasant. I suggest you take it."

"Go to hell."

I fired another bolt. This time, he didn't disappear. He stood his ground and held his hand straight out in front of him. The bolt blinked and vanished before it could reach him. My heart sank, and my frustration started giving way to fear again. Madam Hortence had told me a little about counter-spells, but I thought you had to know a spell to counter it.

"I don't know whether you were just sent as a distraction," he said, "or if she truly believed you had a chance of defeating me. Either way, it was a pointless ploy. I'll know when her bumbling lackeys are getting near, and then I'll be moving on. I've only stayed this long because you fascinate me, and that's owed mainly to morbid curiosity."

I growled in frustration and frantically fired bolt after bolt at him. He casually flicked his wrist toward each one, stopping them with barely any effort. I must have looked pathetic, but if I was lucky he wouldn't guess what I was doing.

I kept firing, until the bolts abruptly stopped. Looking panicked, I tapped on the stone and shook the ring uselessly.

"Come on, come on, don't do this now," I said through gritted teeth. The ring still didn't fire, and I dropped slowly to my knees, audibly sobbing. "Dammit... Why isn't it working?"

The man walked slowly toward me, arms

crossed, a huge grin on his face.

"Having some trouble, are we? Here, let me try."

He leaned down and reached for the ring, just like I hoped. I let him get his hand on mine before I quickly tapped on the band of the ring with my thumb. A bolt of light struck his hand before he could react, and his whole body went limp and tumbled backward onto the floor.

I slowly got up, watching him warily, and inched closer. I could see his eyes were rolled back in his head, and his breathing seemed shallow. I lightly kicked his foot, which remained limp and unresponsive. I allowed myself a little sigh of relief, and smiled.

"Oops. Never mind. Seems like it's working fine now."

For good measure, I pointed and fired once more. His body twitched a little as another bolt struck him in the stomach.

"Yup. Still working. Jerk."

I knelt down beside him and pulled the necklace out of his pocket. The clasp had come undone but wasn't seriously damaged. I stood up and put the necklace back on, smiling to myself. All I had left to do was to wait for the cavalry to arrive. Madam Hortence would be so proud of me.

"Hold it right there!"

I looked up to see another man at the end of the hall by the stairs, pointing a gun at me.

"Show me your hands!" he demanded.

I obeyed, not sure what else to do. He looked me over for a second, then lowered his gun. He pulled a police badge out of his coat pocket and showed it to me.

"It's okay. My name is John Powers. I'm a detective."

He started to walk towards me, then stopped suddenly. His eyes went wide when he saw the man lying on the floor, and pointed the gun toward him.

"What the hell happened here?"

After the ghost slipped through my fingers the first time, I thought maybe I was losing my mind. After he escaped the second time, I was practically sure of it. So were a few other people, if office gossip was any indication. I was just lucky the chief was willing to take a chance on me and my instincts about this guy, and doubly lucky to get a competent intern who didn't ask too many questions.

James wound up being a big help from the start. Reviewing tons of old paper police reports is a pretty mind-numbing task no matter who you are, but he was reassuringly willing to put his nose to the grindstone. He didn't have as good a sense of what he needed to be looking for as I did, but he was a quick study, and just having the extra set of eyes was a big time saver in itself.

The map on my wall became covered with red pins pretty quickly, all marking locations of crimes where my suspect may have been involved. There wasn't any obvious pattern to his movements at first, but as I focused on the map I did start to notice something. He had a tendency to commit a series of thefts around the same small area, then move a few blocks over and start again. Eventually he'd circle back to areas he'd covered before, probably sometime after police had given up investigating. Given that, and given how recent my newest report was, I assumed he was still hanging around his current hunting ground. He had to have a hideout somewhere nearby, assuming he ever stops to rest. Those were fairly big assumptions, but I figured I could trust my instincts on this; they were on a hell of a winning streak.

Friday evening, I decided I was ready to go find him. I let James go home at six, then told the chief I wanted to go downtown to check out a possible lead. We're normally not supposed to go anywhere on police business alone, but the chief allowed it. In fact, for secrecy's sake, he was insistent on it. It made sense, but a part of me still wondered why he'd been so on-board with me on this case.

Even before the promotion, the chief seemed like he gave me a lot of rope to do my own thing. My mother taught me not to look a gift horse in the mouth, which was a weird old-fashioned saying even before her time, but it sort of made sense. When you're handed an opportunity, you don't hesitate or question it too much, or else you might not get another one. I decided not to question him about it, at least for the moment.

I drove downtown to begin my search, not altogether sure where to start. My instincts about this guy hadn't led me astray yet, and right away I was feeling that weird little anxious humming in my brain like every other time he was nearby, but as I slowly patrolled the streets looking for anything out of the ordinary, doubt gradually crept into my mind. Even if I was right that he was hiding out somewhere in this neighborhood, there was no telling where exactly. Plus, even if by some miracle I did find him, he'd probably see me coming and just slip away again like he had before.

Once it got dark enough for the street lights to come on, I needed a break. I stopped to get some gas and a cup of coffee, then sat in my car trying to stay awake until the caffeine kicked in. My eyelids were just starting to feel heavy when I was startled by a bright flash of light in the distance. I sat up straight and peered down the street, hoping to make out what had happened, and a moment later there was another flash, and then another. I almost mistook them for lightning flashes at first, but there was no noise and not a cloud in the sky.

I started my car and drove down the street. The flashes continued over and over. By the time I rounded the corner, I could clearly see where they were coming from. A few people had gathered outside, watching the mysterious strobe light show flashing through the sixth-floor windows of what looked like a condemned apartment building. I didn't need any weird gut feeling to know who was inside. I parked my car nearby, jumped out and flashed my badge to the assembled onlookers, just as another bright flash lit up the area.

"Everybody return to your homes," I said, drawing my gun and racing up the steps into the building.

I bolted through the lobby and up the stairs. When I got to the sixth floor landing, I stepped into a dark hallway and saw two figures, one lying flat on the floor. I pointed my gun at the other.

"Hold it right there!" I shouted. "Show me your hands."

My eyes began to adjust to the darkness as the figure raised their hands. It was a girl, probably about James' age, unarmed, and clearly in the wrong part of town. I lowered my gun and showed my badge.

"It's okay. My name is John Powers. I'm a detective."

She looked pretty shaken. As I walked closer, I got a better look at the man lying on the floor. It was him. Instinctively, I pointed my gun toward him, but he wasn't moving. I looked back up at her.

"What the hell happened here?" I demanded.

"This guy attacked me!" she blurted out, pointing to him. "Yeah. He was trying to mug me or something, but I got the jump on him and I knocked him out."

I raised an eyebrow. "*You* knocked *him* out?"

She shrugged. "I take judo classes. He shouldn't have messed with me. When I'm startled, I'm like a tornado."

She threw a few wild punches into the air to emphasize her point.

"Clearly," I said, unconvinced. "Well, just stay put for a minute."

I walked around checking the rooms on the floor, but they all appeared empty. As hard as it was for me to believe that this small girl took my suspect down by herself, there wasn't anybody else around who could have. Something was definitely suspicious, but I wasn't getting any bad vibes from her like I did from him or the shadows.

"What were those flashes of light earlier?" I asked her.

"Um..." she hesitated, biting her lip. "Oh, that was, uh..."

"Look, you're not in trouble, I just need to know what happened. Did he have a gun?"

"Yes! I mean, n-no..." She stammered a bit. "W-wait, he... it's..." Her face was suddenly getting very pale.

"It's okay, just relax."

"I am... h-he had a..." She seemed be struggling to put the words together. "The lights..."

Her eyes fluttered as the color continued to drain from her face. She was going to faint. I grabbed her by the shoulders just as she started to fall over.

"Woah."

I helped her to the floor and sat her against the wall.

"Hey, what's wrong? Did he do something to you?"

I held a hand to her forehead, and was shocked how hot her skin was to the touch. She seemed fine a moment ago, and suddenly she was running a high fever. She was pale and sweating profusely, and she was getting more delirious by the second, her eyes drifting aimlessly.

"Okay... okay, just stay with me here," I said, trying not to seem panicked. "Who are you? What's your name?"

"V..Vivian..." she managed finally.

"Okay, just sit tight Vivian. I'm going to call for help."

I stood up and made the call to police dispatch. After the operator assured me they'd have an ambulance there in a matter of minutes, I thanked them and turned back to check on Vivian. She wasn't responding to my voice anymore. Her pulse seemed stable for the moment. There had to be more I could do for her, but I was a little rusty on my first-responder training and I didn't want to make whatever this was worse. Also, I couldn't shake the feeling my suspect would slip away again if I took my eyes off him for too long. With help on the way, I decided to leave her alone for the moment and check on the ghost, still lying where I left him.

Looking at him, I was a bit taken aback. In the couple of days since I'd seen him he apparently got a new set of old clothes, and a clean shave too. Same hat as before, though. He definitely seemed unconscious but was breathing steadily, and there were no obvious signs of a struggle. I put on a pair of gloves and searched through his clothes, hoping I might find a wallet or some other personal item to help identify him. In his vest pocket, I found a small leather-bound notebook. It had a black, lightly worn cover, and a miniature pencil was tied to it with a string hanging from its spine. I opened the notebook to the first page.

Don't lose the notebook. Don't lose the notebook. Don't lose the notebook.

That's all that was written, over and over. Puzzled, I flipped to the next page and found the same thing. I flipped ahead a bit further and found a new phrase, again being repeated over and over.

Use everyone, trust no one. Use everyone, trust no one.

It went on like that for several more pages. What struck me was, as strange as the repeated writings seemed, they didn't look like the frantic scribbling I might have expected from someone exhibiting this kind of obsessive behavior. Every line, every letter was meticulously written in an old Gothic-looking style, artfully drawn and perfectly legible. It must have taken him ages to write each page. And then...

Seriously, don't lose the notebook. Seriously, don't lose the notebook.

I kept skimming through, finding similar things. One phrase repeated for two or three entire pages at a time. Every tenth page or so seemed to be dedicated to *Don't lose the notebook.* The rest varied, from callous anti-social statements, to simple instructions, to some things I couldn't make any sense of at all.

Take anything, leave no trace.

Avoid N. Cedar St.

Compassion will kill you.

I don't need anyone. I don't want anyone.

Go below S. 53rd St. Don't stay too long.

Aeternus Excruci – for emergencies.

I am nobody.

*DO NOT get Chinese takeout from Golden
Panda again.*

Don't underestimate the detective.

That last one stuck out. It was toward the end
of the book. The pages after it were all blank. I got out
a plastic evidence bag, slipped the notebook inside
and pocketed it as I stood up. There would be time to
decipher what it all meant later.

I was about to check on Vivian again when I felt
a sudden sharp sting in my mind again, just as intense
as the other night at the station. I looked toward
Vivian, who was fading in and out of consciousness,
fidgeting with her necklace and staring into space. She
cracked a weak smile.

"You made it," she muttered, looking toward the
stairs.

From down the hall, I could just barely make
them out. Shadowy figures appeared from the
stairwell, just like the ones that appeared before, and
they were walking slowly toward us. If my growing

headache and their fuzzy outlines were any indication, there were more of them than before, maybe five or six altogether. I drew my gun and took a few paces toward them, being sure to put myself between them and Vivian.

"That's close enough. Stop where you are," I ordered them, aiming my weapon. They didn't react at first. Then, to my surprise, they halted in their tracks, staring at me with hollow, featureless faces.

"You have fantastic timing, Detective."

It took me a moment to realize the voice had come from behind me. I whirled around and saw my suspect rising to his feet. I trained my gun on him, still trying to glance over my shoulder at the shadows.

"Well, here we are again. Interesting..." he said, brushing his clothes off. He glanced down at Vivian. "What happened to the girl?"

"Like you don't know," I spat.

"I might have a guess..." He started to grin, but stopped and felt his vest pocket. He glared hard at me. "You took my notebook."

"It's evidence in a criminal investigation now."

"You can't just take that. I need it. Give it back."

"I don't think so."

His left eye twitched a bit. He put his hand over his face and inhaled sharply, then let out a heavy sigh.

"Everyone is quite intent on testing my patience tonight, aren't they? Let's be reasonable about this, shall we? That book has no value to you whatsoever. Just give it back to me, before I'm forced to take it back myself."

"Try it."

I held my gun steady, looking down the sights at him. Unless I missed my hunch, he couldn't disappear as long as I had a hold on him, so getting close to me is the last thing he'd want. He kept his eyes locked with mine, unblinking. He didn't look intimidated, but he wasn't coming any closer either.

"Are you going to return my property to me or not?"

"I'll tell you what: come quietly with me back to the station, and tell me exactly what's wrong with the girl. Then maybe you'll get your book back."

"You're in no position to be making demands."

I gritted my teeth, then glanced back at the shadows again. They held still, but I got the feeling they had inched closer while I wasn't looking. I turned my attention back toward the ghost and took a step forward.

"I have back-up on the way," I said. "When they get here, we're taking her to a hospital, and I'm taking you in for questioning."

"A hospital won't do her much good."

He knelt down beside her and took her hand in his, her arm hanging limp at her side.

"Get away from her!" I barked.

He didn't react. His index finger traced delicately over an ornate ring she was wearing, his gaze lost somewhere in the gemstone.

"What are you going to do, Detective? Shoot me?"

"If I have to."

Slowly, he stood up and backed away from her, holding his hands out at his sides. His mouth curled into a sly smirk. He held out his right hand and pointed his index finger at me like a gun.

"Not if I shoot you first."

I thought he was just calling my bluff. I couldn't possibly bring myself to shoot an unarmed suspect; not even him. Not unless there was a credible threat, which I didn't think there was. I should have known better.

"Bang."

As the word left his mouth, I was suddenly blinded by another flash of light. Something hit me in the chest and knocked me flat on my back. I coughed and gasped for air, barely able to hear myself over the ringing in my ears. I tried to pick myself up and get back to my feet, but my body wasn't responding. With numb hands, I desperately felt around the floor for my gun but couldn't find it.

"You can move already? Impressive," I heard him say as the ringing sound subsided.

My vision was slowly returning, and I could see him kneeling down beside Vivian again. I tried to speak, but I'd had the wind knocked out of me and could barely breathe, let alone form words. He turned and looked back at me, still smirking wickedly.

"If you're so interested in my notebook, then keep it for now. When you realize it's worthless to you, bring it to the corner of Clinton and South 53rd. Maybe we can make a trade."

He grabbed her arm, and the two of them vanished. I looked around, and the shadows began disappearing as well. With some effort, I managed to reach my phone, but it slipped from my grasp. As I lay there struggling, I heard his voice in my mind mocking me one more time.

"*You'd better hurry up, Detective. She doesn't have much time.*"

Chapter 8: You're A Wizard

Whatever had hit me, the effects had mostly worn off by the time help arrived. I must have still looked like I'd been hit by a train, because the paramedics were reluctant to let me drive myself home, at least until after they'd checked me out. Unfortunately, I didn't get much rest that night. I was too anxious to find Vivian as soon as possible, even if my body was less willing. James ran up to me the moment I walked in the door early the next morning.

"You're alive!" he beamed. For a second, I thought he was going to hug me.

"I will be after my coffee," I replied, taking a sip from the travel mug in my hand. "Had kind of a long night. I guess you heard that, though."

"There were reports of shots fired in your area, and when I heard you'd called for paramedics I was fearing the worst, you know?"

"Yeah. It's alright, nobody got shot. Things just got a little rough, and I took a hit in the ribs. I'll be fine." The 'hit' in question didn't leave any obvious damage, not even on my clothes, but it definitely left me feeling drained. The three hours of sleep didn't really help with that.

"Still, think of how much worse it could've been. Where was your partner?"

We were almost back to my desk. I glanced around to make sure nobody else was listening before I turned to him and answered, keeping my voice low.

"I don't have one."

"What?" He took the hint and lowered his voice too. "You went out after a dangerous suspect *by yourself?* Can you even do that?"

"Why don't you ask the chief? He's the one who authorized it."

"Seriously?"

I took another gulp of coffee. "I'm going to his office now. Why don't you tag along? I'll introduce you."

"Sure." He smiled nervously. "I've heard a lot about him. People said he's really intense though."

"He can be. You get used to it. Come on."

Chief Riley was generally well-respected in our precinct, but he had a reputation for being stand-offish and especially tough on new guys. The treatment I got from him was pretty out of the ordinary compared to the experience other new detectives got. Most of them compared it to dental surgery.

I knocked on the open door to his office as I stepped inside, with James following just behind me.

The chief was sitting at his desk, arms folded in front of him.

"Powers." His deep, gravelly voice visibly put James on edge.

"Sir. This is James Klein. He's the intern who has been helping me on the case the past couple of days."

"It's an honor to meet you, sir," James added.

"Not getting in your way, is he?" the chief asked.

"Just the opposite," I said. "I doubt I'd have found that lead last night so quickly without him."

"Glad to hear it."

If he was glad, his face didn't hint at it. He stroked his mustache thoughtfully, looking James over.

"So, where do we stand on this now? Are we any closer to ID-ing this suspect of yours?"

"Maybe if the lab could pull DNA or fingerprints off of the notebook I recovered. Any luck there?"

"Last I checked, they hadn't gotten to it yet. There's a bit of a back-up. Mr. Klein, you're studying forensics, aren't you? Why don't you head down there now and see if they could use a hand?"

"Oh, sure thing." James smiled and backed out the door. "It was a pleasure meeting you, sir."

I paused a few seconds after he left and closed

the door before continuing.

"Has there been any word on the missing girl?" I asked him.

"I'm afraid not. It would help if we knew who she was. I wish you had checked her ID when you had the chance; a first name isn't much to go on."

"I know, it was careless of me. I was focusing on the suspect. Besides, I thought she'd still be there when the paramedics arrived."

"How concerned should I be?"

"I don't know. I'm still not sure what caused her to faint. She at least seemed fairly stable the last time I saw her."

"Do you think he'll hurt her?"

I was afraid he might ask that. I had no way of knowing what the ghost's intentions were, so I could only give my best guess.

"Not yet, at least. Nothing in his MO leads me to think he's prone to violence, and he needs her alive if he expects us to make a trade." Negotiating with kidnappers goes directly against policy; I didn't give the chief a chance to remind me. "What choice do we have, really? If I don't give him what he wants, he has no reason to let her go, and if he decides to go into hiding there's no telling when we'll find him again. This is the best chance she has."

The chief stared at me. "Are you sure he'll honor the trade if you go through with it?"

"He'll have to." I tried to say it with some conviction.

He stared hard at me and took a long breath.

"Alright then," he said finally. "Take the notebook out of evidence when you're ready. Don't worry about evidence room procedures, I'll get the paperwork sorted. Ideally we'll pull something useful off it first, but the girl's safety is more important."

"...Okay. Thank you, sir."

I was about to turn to leave, but something was nagging at my mind that I just couldn't let go of.

"Is there something else?"

"Sir... why are you doing all of this? You gave me a promotion just so I could focus on the case I wanted to, you've broken procedure to help me along the way, and you trust all my crazy hunches no matter how shaky the evidence is. Why?"

"Hmm. I'd just assumed you figured that out already. Or at least had a guess."

"Well I don't, so please fill me in. What's your interest in this case?"

He closed his eyes and sighed, then looked at me again and leaned forward, resting his elbows on the desk.

"Before I say anything else, I need to reiterate that what we discuss about the particulars of your case stays between the two of us. Is that understood?"

I nodded. "Of course."

He raised his voice. "Is that understood, Mr. Klein?!"

I heard sudden frantic footsteps in the hallway. I opened the door and leaned out into the hall just in time to see James rounding a corner down the hall. I chuckled to myself, then stepped back inside and closed the door.

"How did you know he was eavesdropping?" I asked.

"You're not the only one with strong intuition," the chief said. He gestured for me to take a seat in front of him, which I did. "It comes in handy in this line of work. Law enforcement needs people like us."

"People like us?"

"You and me. And your suspect. We're different from most people. We can do things they can't because we have access to something they don't. Special abilities, and insight into our environment. In the old days, they might have called it magic."

I furrowed my brow.

"It sounds kind of crazy when I say it aloud,

doesn't it?" he continued. "But then, so does a criminal that can disappear and walk through walls."

"Forgive me sir, but that's just ridiculous. I'm sure you have keen instincts and everything, but what about that is magical?"

"Even people with keen instincts find their gut is wrong from time to time. That's something you and I have never had to contend with."

It occurred to me he might have a point. Offhand I couldn't think of any time my intuition had steered me wrong. That didn't make it magic, though.

"I'm still not buying it."

"Yeah, I didn't think you would. Me and my crazy nonsense." He glanced at the travel mug I still had in my hand. "Is your coffee getting cold?"

"Um... well, yeah. I didn't have time to brew a fresh pot-"

He held out his hand. "Give it here."

"Sir?"

"Come on. It'll just take a second."

Slowly, I handed him the lukewarm cup. He took it, removed the lid, and sat holding it out in front of him. We both looked at the cup, I with a bemused grin, he with unflinching focus. I was about to ask what he was doing when a few wisps of steam began rising from the cup. I watched unblinking as the steam grew thicker, and the liquid started to bubble like it was coming to a boil. He calmly put the lid back on the cup and set it in front of me.

"Nothing up my sleeve," he said, pulling back the cuff of his shirtsleeve for emphasis.

I picked up the cup and found it hot to the touch. My mind strained for the usual logical explanations, but couldn't find one.

"That little trick has come in handy a few late nights. I've always hated cold coffee. Just doesn't feel right on the palate."

"Okay..."

I took a small sip from the mug, then set it back down on the desk. Nothing tasted out of place, but I was a little too freaked out to finish the rest.

"For the sake of argument," I said, "I'll accept the possibility that magic or something like it might exist. If so, why would I have it? What's so special about me?"

"Well, from what little I've found on the subject that sounded credible, this thing seems to run in families, so maybe it's a genetic quirk. Seems to be true for my family, anyway. You know, my grandfather was a great homicide detective; his instincts were always spot-on too. My brother is a detective, and he's got our grandfather's instincts. My father is a retired district attorney, and he always had an amazing knack for knowing when people were lying. This is all just anecdotal, of course."

My eyes wandered toward the floor. "Well, I can't say that sounds like my family. I'm the only one in law enforcement. My mother doesn't have any special talents or intuition or anything. At least she never told me she did. Her brother and her parents are pretty normal too. "

"What about on your father's side?"

"I never knew my father."

"I'm sorry to hear that."

"Don't be," I said quickly. "He ran out on my mom before I was born. She told me he was just a low-life, and we were better off without him. My intuition always said she was right."

"Hmm. I suppose she was."

I cracked a slight smile. "So, where do you get this idea that it's genetic from? What's your source? Where do you even find a credible source on magic?"

"Ah. That's a bit of a story in itself." He leaned back in his chair. "When I first joined the force, I was kind of surprised to find out how rarely cases got tied up neatly, with conclusive evidence and credible witnesses. Most police didn't have the kind of sharp instincts that the ones on TV had, or that my family had. I was curious what made us different, so in my free time I did some research at the library. I tried to find anything about intuition running in families. There were a couple of old psychology studies that suggested something like that, but nothing conclusive."

Producing a key from his pocket, he reached down and unlocked the bottom drawer of his desk as he continued.

"I wasn't satisfied, so I expanded my search to other topics. Psychics, mind-readers, clairvoyants, sorcerers or what-have-you. Most of it was the usual nonsense you might expect. But I found one book that intrigued me."

He pulled a thick, well-worn text book from the drawer and placed it in front of me. The front cover read <u>Mythology of Early European Cultures, 1st Ed.</u> He opened it to the very back where a sort of pocket was built into the back cover, and a much smaller book was tucked inside. This little booklet was missing the front and back covers, reduced to a thin stack of pages bound by their spine, but the pages themselves appeared to be in good condition with minimal signs of wear. He pulled out the booklet and turned the first blank page over to reveal the title, printed in a small Gothic font that looked sort of familiar.

The Humble Mage's Companion:
A Beginner's Guide to the Magical Arts,
by K. L.

"Might've been fate or just dumb luck that this was in the library system at all," he said. "The mythology textbook itself has been out of print almost 50 years, and none of the branches had it in stock. Even if they did, near as I can tell, only a handful of them shipped with this little stowaway tucked in the back. I only have my intuition to thank for leading me to this one; some collector from out of town had it. The guy made me wear gloves to read it. I practically had to promise him my first born son to get him to part with it."

"Why did you want it so badly?" I asked.

"Partly because my intuition told me I needed it, and it hadn't been wrong in ages. Partly because of what I read."

He opened the book to a page in the middle with the corner folded down. There was a paragraph talking about some kind of private school, part of which was highlighted in yellow.

Since only a small fraction of humanity were sufficiently attuned to the world's magical energy to tap into it, only children whose families carried a bloodline granting them the ability to manipulate

magic would be invited to enroll, and their families
sworn to secrecy regardless of enrollment status.

"This doesn't necessarily prove anything," I said.

"You're right, it doesn't. But there are other
sections describing how magic supposedly works, and
from what I've been able to observe, they seem pretty
accurate. How do you think I learned that coffee
trick?"

He flipped back toward an earlier section and
started scanning over the pages.

"Finding out about this ghost of ours reminded
me of another part I'd read a while ago. Here, have a
look at this bit. Anything sound familiar?"

He pointed to the last sentence on the page, but
my eyes were drawn to the paragraph that came right
before it.

There are only two commonly known æthereal
spells suited for combat, one which launches a brilliant
beam of pure æther to render an enemy unconscious
or temporarily immobile, and one which summons a
small invisible barrier of force that may offer some use
as a shield. Due to their basic applications and the
general ubiquity of æther itself, these spells can be
employed by even novice mages with any elemental
attunement. As such, they were traditionally taught to
students of magic early on for use in self-defense or in

the course of dueling. The subject of dueling will be covered in greater detail later in this book.

More potent uses for æther have been discovered in the past, including invisibility, intangibility, and instantaneous transportation, but there is sadly little available knowledge on these subjects.

"Of course it could all just be coincidence," the chief said.

"This sounds like what I got hit with last night." I pointed to the paragraph. "I think he shot some kind of beam at me, and I was laid out on the floor unable to move."

"Son of a gun..." He shook his head, sounding a bit surprised as he spoke. "You think he could have done worse if he wanted to?"

"I don't know. He always seems like he's toying with me. I can't be sure if he's just playing head games or he really knows a lot more than we do."

"Well, I had hoped things wouldn't get this dangerous, or at least this quickly, but it seems like the time has come to bring you up to speed on the basics, at least as far as what this author had to offer, whoever they are. He makes a big deal about 'knowledge and intent', so just staying focused and keeping your wits about you seems to be the biggest part of it. Then there are the spell names, which seem to be Latin words or phrases most of the time."

My mind immediately jumped back to what I'd read the day before in the notebook.

"Why Latin?"

"Probably because it's a dead language. Fewer people in centuries past could read or write at all, but even fewer knew any Latin. If these mages wanted to keep their work secret, that was a pretty good way to do it."

"There was some Latin written in the notebook."

"Any idea what it said?" He didn't sound surprised.

"No. It was just a few words, though. The rest was in English, and I still couldn't really make sense of it."

"Hmm." The chief stroked his mustache again. "If you have time, photocopy the pages. I'd like to take a look myself."

"Sure. Anything that could help, right?"

He nodded and leaned back in his chair. "Anyway, you wanted to know why I trusted you? Because I knew you were like me. The first time we met I could feel that energy radiating off of you. It's not an easy thing to perceive or make sense of, but I've had some practice at it. I'm guessing you have too lately. Don't worry, the headaches and paranoia will pass as you get used to having a sixth sense."

I unconsciously gave a sigh of relief. While I still couldn't be entirely sure what to believe, it at least felt like things were starting to make sense.

"Anyway, I know you're eager to get out there and bring Vivian back. There's just one more thing before I let you go. If you're going to be dealing with people with these kinds of abilities, you'll need some more of your own. I've got at least one new trick I can teach you right now, and it should only take a second."

He grabbed a pen and wrote a word on a piece of paper, then showed it to me and read it aloud.

"Dimitto. Latin word for 'dismiss.' Think of it as kind of a catch-all to get rid of curses and the like. I haven't really had much cause to test it out myself, but I figure it's better than nothing."

I read the word silently to myself. "So, am I just supposed to shout it, like abracadabra or something?"

"Thinking it should be enough, but it can't hurt to say aloud if you're not sure. It's all down to your focus. Also, you'll have to be in direct contact with someone else if you want to use it on them. Otherwise it just affects you."

"Okay. Good to know."

"When there's time, you should give this book a

quick read. I wish I could do more to prepare you for this, but I'm not exactly an expert myself."

"What about the coffee heating trick?"

He grinned. "That one I'll leave you to figure out for yourself. You're dismissed. Good luck out there."

"Okay. Thank you, sir."

I got up and left the room, silently hoping I wasn't in too far over my head.

Chapter 9: Æthereal Jaunt

I couldn't quite remember what happened. I knew I'd caught the guy I was looking for, and I remembered that a detective showed up and started questioning me. I was afraid he'd know if I was lying to him, and that he would find out the truth about why I was there. Then everything got kind of fuzzy.

I woke up to a familiar sight: the guy with the bowler hat. I tried to scramble away, but he had a tight grip on my hoodie. Worse, I realized there was nowhere for me to scramble to. We were floating in a gray void, my arms and legs whirling uselessly. I felt like a cartoon character who'd just run off of a cliff and made the mistake of looking down. The guy looked amused, watching me flail around.

"I wouldn't do that if I were you," he said. "If I lose my grip, you're in for a nasty fall."

"Where am I?" I asked.

"Clinton Street. A few thousand feet above it, to be exact."

I tried to turn in place and look below us, assuming below was the direction his feet were facing. I could just make out the tiny buildings and streets clogged with cars going in every direction. All of it was gray and blurred, like I was looking through a smudged window pane. A few gray blobs that I figured were birds fluttered over the rooftops. Only he and I looked normal.

I felt the magic ring, still on my finger. For a second I considered trying to use it again, but that would have been a big mistake. Knocking him out would probably disrupt whatever enchantment was keeping us both from falling, and I wasn't keen on risking both our lives. Besides, he probably wouldn't have let me keep the ring with its magic still intact.

"How long have I been here?" I asked.

"Not long. Though I suppose time is a relative thing, especially here. In any case, it'll just be the two of us for some time yet, so we might as well get acquainted, don't you think? Perhaps you could start by telling me more about yourself, or about the people in that manor who desperately want me done away with."

I stood my ground (figuratively) and crossed my arms, trying to look brave.

"I don't have anything to say to you."

"Fine." He smirked. "You don't feel like talking? What about screaming?"

He let go of my hoodie, and all at once he and the gray void were gone. The world regained its normal color, and I started falling. I felt my heart leap into my throat. The city below was growing larger, and I started tumbling head over heels. I screamed, but the sound was quickly drowned out by the deafening wind rushing past me. Then, just as quickly as it had disappeared, the gray murky void snapped back into place around me, and I lurched to a stop. I felt two hands tightly gripping my shoulders from behind.

"I'd figured you for a screamer," he said dryly.

I bit my lip to try to keep from crying. My heart had been pounding but it seemed to stop once I was in the gray void of the æther again. I instinctively sucked in deep breaths. Part of me wondered what exactly I was breathing but I tried not to think about it.

"Now, it seems to me that the two of us got off to a bad start," he continued in a mocking tone. "I'd like it if we could be friends, you know? I could really use somebody to talk to, and for the foreseeable future, it's just you and me up here."

"What about Madam Hortence?" I managed to say finally. "She'll look for me. She'll find me."

He laughed. "Do you really expect a dramatic rescue from your precious Madam? Well, please allow me to dissolve that unfortunate delusion for you right now. First of all, if that stupid old hag and her stooges could find and stop me on their own at this point, they wouldn't have needed to send you."

I gritted my teeth, but then stopped. I was expecting to be furious when he insulted Madam Hortence, and was all set to jump into an angry diatribe about how amazing and powerful she is like last time, but nothing came. I was still annoyed with him, but it felt nothing like before.

"Second, Madam Hortence doesn't care enough about you to attempt to rescue you. You were her pawn, nothing more."

"That's not true," I said. "Of course she cares about me."

"How do you know that?"

"Because, she..."

I couldn't finish the thought. There had to be a reason why I trusted her so much, but I couldn't think of it. We both loved the Lewis Building, obviously, but beyond that I barely knew anything about her, and what I did know was just what she'd told me. A terrible doubt crept into my mind, and I wasn't sure if I should fight it.

"She was manipulating you with her charms," he continued, "to make you think and do whatever she wanted. She never gave a goat's beard about you; you were just a toy for her to play with. Do you think she even trusted you? You passed out after the detective showed up because she'd put a curse on you to keep you from talking. She was prepared to kill you just to keep her secret safe."

"That..." I shook my head. "No, that's impossible. She wouldn't do that. *You* must have done something to make me pass out."

"And when did I do that? When I was lying on the floor in a state of paralysis? Hardly my proudest moment, I'll admit, but the point still stands."

I didn't have an answer for that. I couldn't believe Madam Hortence would really kill me to keep me quiet, but at the same time, I knew how important it was to her that nobody else ever learn about her existence. Would she really be willing to kill me to protect herself?

"How do I know you're not making this up?" I asked defiantly, looking back over my shoulder at him. "If magic can be used to control people's minds, how do I know you're not just doing that now to turn me against Madam Hortence?"

He shrugged. "I suppose you don't. That's what's so delightfully devilish about charms. They inject strange thoughts into your head and then convince you that those thoughts were there all along. They're like religious sermons, or advertisements for children's breakfast cereal."

I thought he was just trying to get a reaction out of me. I turned away again.

"Explain this, then: if Madam Hortence tried to kill me, why am I still alive?"

"Oh? You mean you haven't figured it out?"

He pulled me closer, until I could practically feel his breath on the back of my neck. I was fully creeped out, but I didn't want a repeat of what happened the last time he took his hands off me either.

"Obviously, because I need you alive."

I did my best to ignore the major douche-chill alarms going off in my head. I knew he was trying to mess with me. I was so focused on trying to keep up a brave front, it took me a few seconds before I fully got what he was saying.

"Wait... You saved me?"

I worked up the nerve to turn around and push him back. I was careful to get a hold on his sleeve first, though.

"Bullcrap. I was sent by Madam Hortence to capture you. Why would you help me?"

He clicked his tongue. "Such fire..."

As the words left his mouth, his gaze seemed to go blank a moment. I thought he was just staring at me at first, but I got the sense he was actually looking past me. His expression seemed like he was worlds away, lost in a dream. Then he stopped, closed his eyes and shook his head at whatever had crossed his mind.

"In any case," he continued, "you've already gotten plenty of answers out of me. Now it's your turn. I'd like to know more about your Madam Hortence."

"You expect me to betray her?"

"The woman who enslaved your mind with magic, then tried to have you killed when you'd outlived your usefulness? Yes, I expect you to betray her. And before you consider saying no to me again, allow me to remind you..."

He yanked his arm out of my grip, and the world flashed back to normal. My heart leapt again, but this time I barely started to fall before the void returned. He held tight onto my arms, and pulled me up closer so my eyes were level with his.

"In the most literal sense of the phrase, your fate is in my hands. Now what's it going to be?"

I wasn't sure what to think. It seemed like he had to be lying to me about Madam Hortence, but I couldn't be sure which parts were lies and which were the truth, if any. Hesitantly, I looked down at the world below, fidgeting with the necklace Madam Hortence had given me, not that it had much use at that moment. I could see countless people going about their lives, unable to see the random girl and her tormentor floating high above them. I started to think about what my parents must have been going through right then. I wasn't even sure how long it had been since I disappeared, whether I'd barely been gone long enough for them to notice, or so long they'd given up hope.

"Okay..." I said. "What do you want to know?"

"For a start: why do her people live in that old museum?"

"She told me they came to this city a long time ago, looking for a peaceful place to live and to keep the secret to eternal life safe. They picked the Lewis Building. There's nothing really special about it, they just liked it, and when it became a museum it became easier for them to hide in plain sight."

"Where did they come from?"

"They all used to be part of British aristocracy in the 19th century."

He snorted, like he was stifling a laugh.

"What?" I scowled back at him.

"Nothing. How many of them are there?"

I had to take a brief mental head count. "Nine altogether."

"What sorts of magic can they use?"

"I know Madam Hortence can enchant objects

so they can hold spells, like the ones she gave me. I guess you know about those already. If you're telling the truth, I guess she can charm people too. I've seen Mister Harold make inanimate objects move on their own, almost like they were alive. Sir Calvin creates illusions; I think that's how they disguise themselves as mannequins during the day. The rest, I'm not sure. There might be more than that, but that's all I know."

He stared quietly at me a moment, then smiled and nodded.

"Alright. See now, that wasn't so difficult, was it? Betraying someone's trust always comes much easier than we would like to think it does."

"So, are you going to let me go now?"

"Of course not; that would make an awful mess." He glanced down at the street far below. "As for whether you get to go home, that's up to our detective friend at this point."

"What? Why?"

"He has something I want. I offered to make a trade."

I sighed. "So you're just using me to get what you want, too."

"You're a fast learner."

Allowing myself to relax a bit now that the threat of death was less imminent, I rolled my eyes at him. He responded by laughing and putting his arm around me.

"If I know our friend and his thirst for justice, he'll be along soon," he said. "So for now, we wait."

"Well, could we at least find someplace solid to sit down? I don't know how you can stand this ethereal floaty stuff."

He smirked and raised his legs into a sitting position.

"If it's something solid you desire, you needn't look far," he said, patting his lap.

I think my eyes almost popped out of my head. He laughed again and tussled my hair.

"Oh relax, will you? I'm only teasing. As if I'd be fool enough to have any sort of relations with ordinary girls."

I wasn't sure what to say to that. Thankfully he dropped the subject right there. He looked down through the void at the mid-day traffic far below us. He had that distant look in his eye again. I looked down as well, quietly considering my situation. Maybe he liked me enough not to kill me, but I was far from home free. I worried about what would happen if the detective didn't show up, and then about what would happen if Madam Hortence and the others did instead.

I started to feel really hopeless. I lost the only

power I'd been given. I hated the idea of not fighting back, but with these powerful mages butting heads, and me caught in the middle with no power of my own, I was just a step above totally helpless.

Screw this, I thought, like I usually did if things got frustrating. No matter how it felt, I knew deep down I wasn't really helpless. I just needed to be smart about this. My first priority had to be finding out who I could trust now. Assuming I survived long enough, the next time something magical and dangerous happened, I might need somebody to hide behind.

"Let's play a game to pass the time," the guy said. "I spy with my little eye... something gray."

I let out a deep sigh and covered my face with my hands.

James couldn't get any DNA or fingerprints off the notebook. In fact, nobody in forensics could. They said it seemed like the book had never been held by anyone who wasn't wearing gloves. I had James make copies of a few pages in hopes we might get some clues from them later. As soon as he was done, I took the notebook to make the exchange. There was an abandoned parking lot next to the intersection where we were supposed to meet. I parked my car there and sat in the driver's seat for a while, waiting for the ghost to show up.

After a few minutes, I started wondering if this was all just a setup. Maybe he was just counting on me to be gullible enough to bring back his precious notebook, and as soon as I got out of the car he'd appear, knock me out again and steal back the notebook. It could even be worse than that. Maybe I'd misjudged him altogether, and Vivian was already dead. I tried to put that thought out of my mind.

I took a sip of coffee from my travel mug. It was already getting cool. I didn't have time to freshen it up before I left the station. Thinking about what I'd seen in the chief's office, I twisted the lid off and peered inside. Magically reheating coffee; he'd made it look easy enough. I focused on the liquid in the mug, trying to will it to warm up. Nothing seemed to be happening. The chief had said something about knowledge being necessary, so maybe there was just some trick I needed to know. Then again, he seemed to be implying I could just figure it out on my own.

I thought maybe I just wasn't focusing hard enough. My intuition usually came through for me as long as I stayed focused. I took a deep breath and closed my eyes. I imagined the coffee in the mug, pictured it clearly in my mind. I'd heard in a chemistry class that temperature is basically just how much energy and movement there is in the molecules of something. The faster they are moving, the hotter it is. I pictured the individual molecules of liquid in the mug, watched them being energized, taking off and colliding with each other, all moving around faster and faster, until the whole thing was boiling over.

I opened my eyes. Nothing had changed.

"Damn."

I set the mug down in the cup holder, shaking my head.

"What happened?" James poked his head up from the backseat.

"Nothing, I was just daydreaming."

"I thought maybe you saw the suspect."

"Not yet. Keep your head down, I don't want him seeing you. He's going to think I came alone like last time. I want him to go on thinking that."

"Well, okay. I just wanted to see him is all."

"You don't need to see him. All you need to do is stay out of sight and call for backup if things go wrong."

James begrudgingly hunkered back down on the floor behind my seat.

"Well, how am I supposed to know if things go wrong if I can't see anything?"

"If you hear screaming or gunshots, things went wrong."

"...Okay."

That probably came out sounding colder than I meant it to. I turned around to face him.

"Look, I really don't think it'll come to that, but it's better we play it safe. It's easier to do that if you stay out of sight. Got it?"

"Okay, boss. I'll be ready to make the call if you need me to."

"Thanks, James."

I wasn't lying to him. As time went on, I slowly regained confidence that our guy would show up and honor the trade. Even without my intuition, the more I thought about it, the less likely it seemed to me that he would try to hurt me or Vivian. All of the crimes I had him pegged for were non-violent. Kidnapping would be the most severe crime he'd committed up to this point, at least to my knowledge. And the worst he'd done to me so far was to leave me sprawled out on the floor for a few minutes.

That night, I assumed he'd done something to Vivian that made her pass out, but she was fine when I got there. She didn't collapse until right before those shadows showed up. Whatever those things were, I might have a lot more to fear from them than from him. Vivian seemed to know something about them, and maybe about my suspect. It's possible she had all the missing pieces I needed to complete this puzzle. Assuming she was okay...

Looking across the parking lot and the nearby street, I couldn't see anyone around. James and I seemed to be alone. I wasn't feeling anything out of the ordinary either.

"He still isn't showing himself. I'm going to get out and look around a bit."

I stepped out of the car, holding the notebook still wrapped in a clear plastic evidence bag. I closed the door, and there he was, appeared out of thin air about ten feet away. Vivian was there too. His arm was draped casually around her shoulder. She looked scared but healthy. Healthier than the last time I'd seen her at least.

"Vivian? It's me, Detective Powers. Are you hurt at all?"

"No, I'm... I'm okay."

He grinned. "You certainly took your time getting here, but that's fine. The young lady and I have been getting to know each other. I kind of enjoy her company, actually. If you're not finished with the notebook you stole from me, I'd be happy to keep her a little longer."

"I'm all ready to trade. The notebook for the girl, like you said, right?" I held up the notebook. "So, how do you want to do this?"

He fell silent for a moment, looking past me. "Well, that's odd. I really thought you would've come alone."

I tried to hide my surprise and anxiety. I don't think I succeeded. He really spotted James that fast?

"It's alright, I never said you had to. I'm somewhat perplexed by your choice of backup is all."

I sighed. "I told the kid to keep out of sight."

"He has, for the most part. I'm just slightly more perceptive than he is covert."

I swallowed a lump I felt forming in my throat.

"Alright, are we doing this or not?" I asked.

"I'm ready if you are, Detective."

I slowly took a step forward. He did the same. I took another step, and so did he, keeping Vivian close. We kept inching closer that way. I held out my hand to Vivian, urging her toward me. He held out his hand for the notebook.

"I don't want any tricks."

"Neither do I."

I kept my eyes locked on his, and he did the same back to me, still grinning. He seemed to take pleasure in how tense he was making me. With each passing moment, I kept thinking he was just about to suddenly snatch the notebook from my hand and disappear with Vivian again. If he did, I wasn't sure I could be quick enough to stop him. That didn't mean I couldn't try.

I beckoned to Vivian, and she held out her hand to meet mine. Our fingers were just about to meet, and he suddenly grabbed the notebook. I started to lunge forward, but instead of abruptly pulling away like I expected, he nonchalantly pushed Vivian toward me and stepped back. A wave of relief slowly washed over me, even as I instinctively grabbed her by the shoulders. I was still half-expecting both of them to vanish into thin air again.

"You're okay," I said. "He didn't do anything to hurt you, did he?"

She shook her head, then looked up at me. "What day is it?"

"Saturday. You've been gone since last night."

She sighed and smiled slightly. "My parents think I was staying over at a friend's house. They probably haven't even missed me yet."

I looked over at the ghost as he tossed aside the empty evidence bag and began flipping through the notebook. He looked up at me and shook his head disapprovingly.

"Honestly, I just can't get over it. A lawman who steals? How shameful."

With that, he was gone, blinked out of existence just as suddenly as he'd appeared. The whole time he'd been standing there, I never felt anything different. Whatever magic ability allowed me to feel his presence so far, he seemed to know how to hide himself from it now. Trying not to dwell on that terrifying prospect, I walked Vivian back to the car. She said she was fine, but she still seemed distant. We got into the car and James sat up in the backseat.

"Hey, we did it! Nice work, boss."

I gave James a weak smile, then turned to Vivian, who was still staring off into space.

"I know you've been through a lot, but can you tell me anything about what happened? Do you know who that guy is? Did he say anything to you?"

"Look, I'm just..." She wiped her eyes, though it didn't seem like she'd been crying. "Can we not talk about this right now? I just kind of... I really want to go home now."

"Alright, that's fine. We just need to head back to the station first. I need to file a report. And you should really be looked over by a doctor just in case."

"I told you, I'm fine."

"Even so, it's a standard protocol thing. Don't worry, we'll get you home soon, trust me."

She leaned against the car door, gazing out the window.

"I'll try."

We had Vivian checked out by a doctor, and she was given a clean bill of health, though the doctor obviously noted she seemed to be under a lot of stress. As soon as she was cleared to go, we headed back to the station. I had the unpleasant job of calling Vivian's parents to let them know where she was. Her mother sounded close to fainting when I told her I was calling on behalf of the police department. I assured the two of them that their daughter was fine and wasn't in any trouble, we just wanted to get a statement from her. I would call them back when she was ready to go home.

Once I got off the phone with them, I went to the chief's office to quickly update him on the situation, then headed back to my desk. James was there waiting for me. I had left him with Vivian in the interrogation room, thinking maybe she'd be more comfortable talking to somebody closer to her own age. Judging by the look on James' face, I thought wrong.

"Anything?" I asked.

"I got her a hot chocolate." He tilted his head, gesturing toward the interrogation room down the hall.

"She's not saying anything. She wasn't really all there. Sorry, boss."

"It's alright. And you don't have to call me boss. You're not technically my employee."

"I know. I don't mean it literally, it's just something you call someone who you respect. You know, an honorific or whatever."

"Okay, then thanks I guess." I shrugged sheepishly. "I'm still getting used to having people answer to me."

"Oh, I do have some good news." He held up a few sheets of paper. "You requested the arrest record on our guy from the other night? They finally sent it over. Fingerprints and all."

"Perfect. Then you have your next assignment: do whatever you can with those prints. With a guy like this, I doubt he'll have any priors in this city, but even if the prints are a dead end it'll still be good practice for you. Besides, and I mean no offense, but I'd rather have you doing your thing here than going out in the field with me anymore."

"You didn't like having to babysit the intern, huh?" He frowned mockingly.

"I just don't want to put you in harm's way. I'm afraid this case is getting dangerous and I'd rather not have to worry about you."

"Sure, I see how it is. Give me just a taste of the real action, then stick me behind a desk to do the grunt work."

He hung his head in mock self-pity. I chuckled.

"Hey, I was stuck behind a desk way longer than you. You'll get no sympathy from me there. Just keep your head down and do your best. You're a smart guy. As long as you work hard you'll get your chance to shine before you know it."

"If you say so..." His tone suddenly became more serious. "Just... look, you know you can trust me, right?"

I was a bit taken aback by the question. "Uh, yeah, sure."

"I'm just saying whatever is going on with this case, you don't have to keep me in the dark about it. I can keep a secret too, you know."

I bit my lip slightly. The chief was pretty clear; no one else was to know about the true nature of our suspect.

"I mean, I don't know what it is, but something's going on." He held up a folder from my desk. "I've looked at your files. Before this kidnapping, the only things you've suspected this guy of were petty theft and burglary. Even if you add them all up, there are guys out on probation who've stolen more than this. So there must be something else going on with this guy. Come on, what is it?"

"James... Look, it's not that I don't trust you. This case is sensitive for a few reasons. I can't really explain it, and if I tried you'd think I was nuts anyway. Look, if things get to a point where I think you need to be in the loop, then I'll explain everything. Until that time, it's probably safer that you not be too involved."

James rolled his eyes. "Fine, be that way. I'll figure it out on my own soon enough."

I laughed halfheartedly, thinking he might just be right.

"Well, I'm going to try to talk to Vivian one more time before I take her home. Get to work on those prints."

He gave me a thumbs-up. "Sure thing, boss."

I walked down the hall to the interrogation room. As I walked, an odd sensation suddenly started clouding my mind. I wasn't sure what it was at first, until the feeling grew into the sharp stinging pain I remembered all too well. I could feel it emanating from the interrogation room. I sprinted the rest of the distance to the room and threw open the door.

"Vivian?"

I stepped halfway through the doorway and stopped dead. Vivian was slumped over the table. Her face was deathly pale, her eyes wide open and out of focus. She didn't look like she was breathing. I could just make out the outline of the shadow looming over her. It seemed to look up at me as I entered the room.

I bolted around the table, grabbed Vivian by the arm and pulled her away from the shadow. She was in no condition to stand on her own, so I lowered her to the floor. Sitting her up against the wall, my mind raced to recover the word the chief had taught me earlier.

Dimitto! Dimitto! I urged, clasping her hand tightly in mine. After an agonizingly long second, she gasped and her eyes snapped open. The color immediately started returning to her face.

"W-what just...?" she stammered, trying to catch her breath.

I looked up at the shadow, which hadn't moved. I held out my hand toward it, trying to bluff some impressive magical attack that I didn't actually possess. It didn't feel very convincing, but the shadow didn't seem to want to take a chance. It stepped backward slowly and faded from view, the pain in my head subsiding as it went. I sighed and lowered my hand.

"Okay, what's going on?" Vivian asked, wiping sweat from her forehead. If she knew she was at death's door a moment ago, she wasn't showing it.

"Did you see it?"

"See what?"

"That... shadow thing." I pointed to where it had been. "I just walked in here to find it staring at you. You were passed out again like before. "

There was a flash of recognition in her eyes. "They came back?"

She looked around the room, grasping at her antique necklace, apparently expecting something to happen.

"Just one," I said. "It's gone now, I think."

"Hmph," she grunted disapprovingly. "Probably thought they'd only need one to finish me off."

She rose to her feet, and the anger in her eyes slowly turned to confusion.

"So wait, who saved me?" she asked.

"Well, I did, I guess."

Her head whipped back around to face me. "You can use magic?"

I blinked. "You *know about* magic?"

"Yeah. I mean, sort of. It's kind of a long story. But you can dispel curses?"

"I guess so." I shrugged. "I'm a little new at this. I'm just relieved it actually worked. If I'd been any slower getting here, I don't know what might have happened."

Vivian looked around once more, then down at her necklace and sighed.

"I guess he was telling the truth after all."

"Who?"

"The creep with the hat."

I stared intently at her. "You talked to him? Why didn't you say anything before?"

"Look, I kind of just found out that somebody I used to idolize has been trying to kill me, okay? Sorry if I wasn't dying to talk about it right away."

"I- okay, I'm sorry. I wasn't trying to be insensitive."

She shook her head and looked up at me sympathetically.

"Listen," she said, "I understand you're looking for answers. But I've had a pretty messed up twenty-four hours. Right now, all I really want to do is go home and see my family, and maybe try to get my head around whatever the hell just happened. But once I've done that, we can talk about what I know. Deal?"

I nodded. "Sounds good. Come on, let's get you home."

Vivian's parents were understandably shaken by the news their daughter had been taken hostage by a fleeing criminal, but they were relieved to see her home safe. I assured them they didn't have anything to worry about, it was just a case of wrong place, wrong time. On the drive back to her suburban home, Vivian had asked me not to mention anything concerning magic to her parents; they weren't in the know. I agreed it probably wouldn't be wise to involve them.

Once she'd had some time to settle in, I asked to speak to Vivian in private. She'd gone up to her room earlier, and her parents agreed to stay downstairs out of earshot. I realized when I got upstairs I had forgotten to ask which room was hers, but I correctly guessed that the door with the colorful "Wizard's Chambers" sign was her room. I knocked on the door.

"It's me," I said.

"Come on in."

I opened the door and stepped inside. Vivian sat at her desk, furiously typing something into her laptop. I sat on the edge of her bed, making some room amid the piles of clothes and a forest of stuffed animals. The only other chair was piled high with books.

"Just give me a sec," she said. "I'll be right with you."

"You're doing homework at a time like this?"

"Of course not, I finished all that ages ago. This is a journal I'm keeping on all this magical stuff. I've been working on it for months, but it's more important now than ever."

I looked around the room as she typed, trying to see how many of the musicians and fictional characters I could recognize in the posters on the walls. Not many, as it turned out, but it struck me how many of them looked like they were before my time. There was one band poster that I was pretty sure I'd seen in my mom's old apartment at one point.

Vivian finished typing a sentence and turned to me.

"Alright, so what do you want to know?" she asked.

"Let's start with this: how are you connected with my suspect? What were you doing there when I found you last night?"

"I was sent to capture him by a woman who used magic to mind-control me. She wanted him caught because he discovered her secret society of ancient mages, and if she let him get away he might reveal to the outside world that they possess the secret to eternal life."

I must have looked like a four-year-old having trigonometry explained to him.

"Sorry..." she said sheepishly. "Maybe I should start from the beginning?"

"Yeah, that would be good."

Vivian proceeded to tell me how she had met Madam Hortence and her people about a year ago, how they had taught her about magic. She went on to explain how Madam Hortence had asked her to catch their intruder, and then how he had delighted in turning her world upside-down, literally and figuratively. She was a little sparse on the details but went over all the relevant things he had told her. As much as the whole story was to take in, I think I was most floored by the revelation that he had saved her life.

"I really thought Madam Hortence was my friend," she said. "She was like my mentor. Then she starts to worry about her people's secret getting out, and what does she do? She tries to kill me with a curse to keep me quiet. Twice! I just feel so stupid."

"If we choose to believe what the ghost told

you, it sounds like it wasn't your fault. You couldn't have known they were controlling you. But how do you know he was even telling the truth?"

"You should have seen him when I talked about Madam Hortence. He was practically laughing in my face, like he couldn't wait to let me in on the big joke. I was mad, but at the same time I felt different than before, almost like waking up from a dream. All the love and admiration and trust I had for Madam Hortence just wasn't there anymore."

"And there's no way he could have put that curse on you himself?"

"I'm positive he was still knocked out the first time I got hit with that curse. But even if he wasn't, the second time in the interrogation room he was nowhere to be seen, but you know who was there? Sir Calvin, one of Madam Hortence's people. His face is the last thing I remember seeing before I passed out."

"Wait, are you talking about the shadow?"

"Yeah. I was confused at first when you said that, but I think I get it now. You can't see into the æther, can you? You just sense the presence of magic nearby, which someone traveling through the æther would definitely be giving off. So, with Sir Calvin and the others, you wound up getting the sense of somebody there without actually being able to see them, right?"

I nodded. She held up her necklace.

"I can actually see them thanks to this. Or at least I could until now. Crazy and manipulative as she is, Madam Hortence really was teaching me about magic. But even if I know how to use magic, I still can't do it without enchanted items like this."

It was becoming clear to me pretty quickly that Vivian's knowledge of magic went way beyond what the Chief had shared with me so far. It was possible she already knew more than both of us. I didn't want to betray his confidence, but I also knew he was eager to acquire all the knowledge we could get on the situation before anyone else could get hurt. In the interest of pooling our knowledge as much as possible, I gave her an overview of what the Chief had told me about magic, and his theory that it must be limited to people with certain bloodlines. Out of respect, I did neglect to mention the identity of the person who told me these things, as well as the book he had drawn some of these conclusions from.

"I guess it makes sense," she said. "If magic is something innate you either have or don't, it would explain how so few people know about it, and why I could never seem to cast my own spells."

"Alright, so this ether... Am I saying that right?

Aether?"

She shrugged. "Close enough."

"So, this aether is how he disappears all of the time?"

"Right. Madam Hortence's books were a little vague on this, but I think I get the gist of it. I don't know how much you know about old theories on the four elements, but the basic idea is that æther is the fifth element, and the most pervasive element of our world. It's like this big blanket of nothing that connects everything else. Even in a vacuum, there's still æther. It occupies the same space as other matter, but things made of physical matter can't really interact directly with the æther or vice-versa. So if you could use magic to turn your physical body into æther, nobody could see or hear you, you could pass through solid objects, and flying becomes the only way to get around because there's no gravity and no solid ground to put your feet on."

I started thinking back to the night the ghost escaped from his cell at the police station.

"So, say someone was in the aether right in front of me, and I couldn't see them, but I reached out and grabbed them."

"You couldn't. Not without using magic, anyway."

"Huh..."

Another theory of mine was beginning to gain traction: even without formal training or knowledge of spells, it seemed like I was sometimes using magic without even realizing I was doing it.

"Okay," I went on, "so the shadows I've been seeing were all Madam Hortence's people. But then why don't I see a shadow when my suspect disappears?"

"Hmm... Maybe because he's crazy fast? I mean, even when I used the necklace, he was just a blur half the time. I think he's had a lot more experience with æthereal travel. Madam Hortence and the others just picked up the spell recently, so they're not as good at getting around without physical bodies. Of course, if he knows how your magic-sense thing works, he could just be resisting it too."

And with that, she confirmed my fear from earlier. That ability to sense his presence was all that enabled me to find him so far. If he knew how to avoid detection now, I might never find him again.

She looked at me intently. "Am I making sense?"

"Mostly, yeah."

"Well... " Her face grew more serious. "Mind if I ask you something?"

"Sure."

"Why is it so important for you to find this guy? What has he done exactly?"

"Petty thefts mostly, as far as I know." I sighed. No point in holding anything back now, I figured. "For me, it's not really about what he did. I just feel like I'm supposed to catch him and I'm not completely sure why. Maybe it's just that he keeps getting away with whatever he wants and I seem to be the only one interested in stopping him. And in the course of chasing him, I stumbled into this whole world of magic, and suddenly the Chief is putting all his faith in me. I want to catch this guy to prove I'm not in over my head. Above all though, my intuition says this guy's important somehow, so I need to catch him and find out more about him. And whoever he is, I'm not about to let him off the hook for his crimes, even if he might have saved your life."

"I know. But you don't think he's dangerous, do you?"

I still didn't have a definitive answer to that question. Between what I'd seen with my own eyes and what Vivian was telling me, I felt like I knew even less about my suspect than I did to start with. With all that had happened, he had to be more powerful than I originally thought. Still, nothing about him so far really gave me the impression of a killer. In fact, he'd had multiple chances to kill me or Vivian for getting in his way, and he didn't take them.

"No," I said finally. "I don't think he is."

"Well, Madam Hortence and her people definitely are. I was so mad when I realized what they'd done, but I knew I didn't have any way to fight back." She grinned. "At least, I didn't before. But now I have you."

"Me? What am I supposed to do?"

"You've got magic, and you're a cop. I was a victim of attempted murder. You need to be the long arm of the law or whatever. Show them that having magic doesn't mean they can just get away with doing whatever they want, like you said."

"I'm already trying and failing to do that with one guy. How am I supposed to go after a whole group of people with magic? I'm not some amazing wizard, I'm just a rookie detective and a rookie magic user. I can't even boil coffee right."

"Don't sell yourself short," she said, grinning. "You can dispel curses; that's pretty huge. And not only that." She held up the necklace again. "This was working right up until you saved me, and then it stopped. I'm betting your spell isn't just for curses, it dispels enchantments in general. That's a crazy powerful spell for a newbie mage. And who taught it to you?"

"Well... I kind of have a mentor, I guess."

The chief wouldn't be happy with me volunteering too much information without checking with him first. I figured I could at least keep his name out of it for the moment.

"Perfect! So we've got *two* mages on our side. That should be enough to handle a few stuffy old people in Victorian clothes. And let's not forget our other powerful asset: me!"

She enthusiastically pointed to herself with both thumbs.

"You?"

"I've worked in the Lewis Building for over a year. I know it inside and out, and I know all the people in Madam Hortence's group. I even know a few of their spells. I could teach you and you'd be able to counter them when they try to use them on you."

"I thought you couldn't use magic."

"I can't, but I can study like a beast. I know some of the spell names and the ins and outs of how they work. That should be all you and your mentor will need to figure them out for yourselves."

"I don't know about this... What about the mind control magic? I'm sure Madam Hortence never taught you that spell. We'd be powerless against it."

"But... well, maybe you could just resist it? I mean especially if you go in expecting her to cast it, you'd only have to resist long enough to dispel it. We'll be fine. Just keep tapping that 'dispel' button when we get inside. It's not like it costs you anything."

I shifted in my seat slightly, trying to avoid sitting on a purple unicorn. I had to admit she made some good points, and a threat like Madam Hortence's group isn't something we could just ignore. But I wasn't nearly as confident as she was about my abilities. It was possible the chief would agree with her and want to pursue these people sooner rather than later, but I didn't want to get her hopes up.

"Look," I said. "I do want to help you. These people sound like really bad news. I'll take everything you told me to my mentor and see what he thinks, but I'm not optimistic about our chances of taking them down. Even if it goes well, they all have this aether they can use to escape, so how are we supposed to capture them all and keep them locked up?"

She shrugged. "I don't know. That hasn't stopped you from chasing your guy, has it?"

"Fair point." I stood up. "Well, whatever he decides, I'll let you know. Thanks so much for all your help."

"Sure thing, and thank you too, Detective Powers."

I offered her a handshake, which she accepted.

"I think this is the beginning of a beautiful friendship," she said with a smirk.

"Uh... okay?"

She saw my puzzled look and rolled her eyes.

"Oh come on, you have to know what movie that's from. It's a classic."

"Sorry, I guess I'm not much of film buff."

"Weak."

I spent the rest of my Saturday night in the chief's office, going over everything Vivian had told me. He seemed to have a better grasp on the situation than I did. He was also understanding about how much information I shared with her, but didn't seem eager to tell her everything just yet.

"Well," the chief said, leaning back in his seat, "what Vivian's shared with you confirms some fears I was having. If these people from the museum are as dangerous as they seem, I'm going to need you to shift your priorities and focus on them. Unfortunately, I'm not sure how to even start making arrests in a case like this. I can't just send you in blind without backup and outnumbered. For now, you'll have to investigate them as best you can and see if we can't get some plan of attack together."

"Maybe we should have put Vivian in protective custody. If they've tried to kill her twice already, they're bound to try again."

"I'm afraid we can't do that. At least not in the traditional way. It would conflict with the cover story we gave about the kidnapping. Besides, the only person who could be much use protecting her is you, and I need you working on this case."

"But I can't just leave her defenseless."

"Don't worry, you won't have to. Here, I've got another arrow to add to your quiver."

He pulled out another piece of scrap paper and passed it to me across the desk. The paper had a new Latin word written on it.

"Aspicio," he said, doing a better job with the pronunciation than I would have. "With this, you can close your eyes and instantly see any familiar person or place you want, no matter where you or they are at that exact moment. Fifty feet or five hundred miles, you'll be able to see them like you're in the same room. So, anytime you want to check on our witness, just close your eyes and think 'Aspicio Vivian' to see how she's doing."

I stared at the word with wonder. "That's incredible... if it works."

"Oh, it works. I've used it a few times to keep tabs on my people around here."

"Okay. But how does that help me protect Vivian?"

"You can do more than just look in on people with this. Once you're seeing them, you can cast more spells at the spot you're looking at. If she's ever in trouble again, she can call you for help on your phone, and then with this spell you can send her a Dimitto from across town if needed."

That paper started feeling a bit heavier in my hand, though maybe it was just in my mind. I closed my eyes for a moment and thought *Aspicio Vivian*, with the intention of seeing her. Almost immediately, I saw an image of her and her parents sitting down to dinner together in their dining room. It looked just as if I were standing in the room with them, although the angle was higher than what I was used to. Seeing that kind of scene always felt a little bittersweet for me, but I was glad to see she was still okay. I opened my eyes and returned my focus to the chief.

"How long have you had this?" I asked.

"Not long. If you couldn't tell, I'm still learning this stuff myself. But it's only useful with people and places I'm pretty familiar with, so it doesn't always work for finding suspects. I tried it on your ghost earlier and couldn't get anything. Speaking of whom, did you see these pages from that nut's notebook?"

He opened a folder sitting on his desk and held up one of several photocopies that James had taken.

"The words Aeternus Excruci appear on this page. I'm not well-versed in Latin, but I don't like the sound of that. And now on top of him we've got this group of supposed immortals willing to kill to keep their existence a secret. I'm beginning to think we may be biting off more than we can chew here."

"Do you think they're really immortal? Is that even possible?"

The chief sighed heavily, putting the photocopies away.

"At this point," he said, "I'm not sure what to believe. Every time I start to think I have a handle on what's real and what's possible, something new comes along and forces me to rethink everything. One thing I'm sure of is that we can't take these people lightly. We're going to need a precise plan of action if we hope to apprehend them without anyone getting hurt."

I nodded my agreement. "So what do you need from me?"

"For now, I want you to find out whatever you can about this Lewis Building's history, and keep talking to Vivian. Learn absolutely everything you can from her about these people, what they can do, and maybe what we can use against them. With any luck, we'll find a way to handle this group before they even know we're onto them, maybe even without exposing them to the public."

"Understood, sir."

I looked down at the scrap of paper in my hand again. I was starting to feel a little more confident that

I'd be able to handle this. But as grave as the situation with these immortals was, someone else still occupied my mind.

"What about my suspect, the ghost?" I asked.

"You're going to have to put that case on hold."

He handed me the folder with the photocopies from the notebook. I think he could sense my disappointment.

"I know you've put a lot of work into tracking him so far, but given the threat to Vivian's life and maybe others, this situation has to take precedent. We're already going to be poking a hornet's nest here. I'd rather not risk poking two at once."

I nodded. "Okay. I understand."

"Alright, you have your assignment. Get to it."

"Yes, sir."

As I walked back to my desk, I weighed the situation in my mind. Logically, with what we had already uncovered about this Madam Hortence and her group, and the things they were capable of, there was no reason for me to dwell on the ghost anymore. Still, he wouldn't leave my mind. I had to assume it was just because I'd spent so much time focusing on him so far. It certainly felt anticlimactic to just drop the case after all that work. But with people's lives at stake, he was just going to have to wait.

My mind then returned to the scrap of paper, which I had stuffed in my pocket in case I forgot the word. If this spell really worked like it seemed to, then the Chief just handed me a very easy way to instantly violate the fourth amendment. I was a little unnerved that he had just handed me something so powerful without setting any real boundaries for its use in an investigative capacity. Maybe he just trusted me enough to assume I wouldn't go spying on people without probable cause. After all, if he didn't trust me but gave me the spell anyway, it would be pretty hard to prove it had ever been used for ill intent. I think I was even more unnerved when it occurred to me just how readily I had used this newfound power with barely a second thought. It called to mind an old saying about power and corruption...

"There you are!"

I nearly jumped out of my skin as James appeared in front of me, grinning ear to ear.

"Oh, hi James."

"You know, I was pretty annoyed you wouldn't tell me what's going on with your case, but it's okay. I've been busy digging, and now I totally get it. You were right; if you had told me yourself, I might have thought you were crazy. Or I mean, some people definitely would have. Not me though. I'm pretty plugged into this stuff myself. Not that I'd expect you to know that about me. My life's not an open book or anything."

He was racing again. I held up my hands.

"James, slow down. What are you talking about?"

"It's okay, boss. You don't have to hide anything from me anymore. I figured it out, and I gotta say, this is huge. My mind has been fully blown."

I furrowed my brow, trying not to look panicked. I had to think he couldn't possibly have figured out the secrets behind this case on his own. Nothing in my case notes made any mention of magic. Some robberies had pretty mysterious circumstances, but that was nothing to go on. Nothing Vivian told me was in writing, and he couldn't have heard anything the chief and I talked about without the chief noticing. At least, I didn't think he could.

"Alright," I said, "let's just step back a second. What exactly do you think you've found out?"

James was holding a folder with a few pages clipped to the inside. He opened the folder and held it up, displaying a grainy black-and-white photograph of the ghost, bowler hat and all.

"This is your guy, isn't it?" He beamed, seeing the recognition in my eyes. "Hah! I knew it. I totally figured it out."

"James..."

Genuine concern was finally setting in. Where could he have dug up a photo of the ghost? What else did he find out? James leaned in close and lowered his voice.

"You're hunting a *vampire*."

"...What?" I stared at him blankly.

"It makes perfect sense. That's why there's all the secrecy and-"

"James, hang on. Even if we pretend for a second that vampires are real, we haven't tied this guy to any violent crimes."

"That doesn't mean anything. He might just be really good at hiding the bodies. Or he's found a sustainable blood source that lets him feed without killing."

"Also, half of what I have on this guy are convenience store robberies, and not just cash, but merchandise too. Why would a vampire need to steal soft drinks and salty snack foods?"

James blinked several times. In his excitement, that thought had apparently been lost on him.

"Uh... damn, I don't know, maybe he's on a diet? Or he has hungry thralls to feed or something?"

"Alright, better question: why would you think

he's a vampire in the first place?"

"Because, he's... well here, look at this stuff."

The two of us continued walking back to my desk. I looked around to confirm nobody had heard our conversation. A custodian gave me a confused look. I shrugged in response. When we got back to my desk, James set the folder down and spread its contents out in front of me.

"I was looking into those fingerprints like you told me. When I searched for a match, the system was turning up nothing. I even expanded the search into other districts, and still nothing. But that didn't add up. If this guy's a career criminal like you're thinking, he had to have some prior arrest at some point, even if he never got convicted. As good as he is now, nobody is perfect when they're first starting out."

"Makes sense..." I added. "But if he started when he was a minor, those records could be sealed by now. And we don't really have any reason to believe his career in crime started here."

"Maybe not. But from the pattern you established, it seems like he has been doing his thing here for years now, maybe decades, and I couldn't believe he never slipped up all this time. So I decided to go on one of the old terminals and get into the legacy system. I know, it's kind of slow and not too reliable, but it did turn up a few partial matches from older records. I went back in the file room and pulled the files from those old arrest records, and guess what I found in one of them? That picture."

I looked at the picture again. It was definitely my suspect, no question. The report it was paper-clipped to appeared to be part of an unsolved homicide investigation, which was far from reassuring.

"Well James, that's some great work, but how-"

"He looks the same in that picture, doesn't he? It's just like the sketch you had made."

"Yes, it's definitely him. What's your point?"

"Why do you think I had to go into the legacy system to find any trace of that prior arrest? You see what the date is at the top of that report? June 6th, 1935. *Thirty-five.*"

I looked at the files James had retrieved, thinking it had to be a mistake. I didn't think the department still had records from that long ago. Even if I chose to believe the date was wrong, the pages of the report looked as though they had aged for decades at least, and I was pretty sure they were photocopies rather than the originals. Also, the mugshot was in black and white. I'm not sure how long ago the police department switched to color mugshots, but it was long enough that neither James nor I would have even been born yet, and the ghost looked like he hadn't aged a day since the photo had been taken. I considered whether the man in the photo could have just been a relative of his or something, but that wouldn't explain the partial fingerprint match, or that he seemed to be wearing the exact same hat.

"So..." James leaned closer again. "If he's not a vampire, just what is he?"

"I don't know. That's what I want to find out." I sighed. "But it's going to have to wait."

"What? Why?"

"I was just coming to tell you, there's been a big development. New case, new suspects, and people's lives might be at risk. It's our top priority starting right now."

"Wow. Yeah, okay. What do you need me to do?"

"Ever heard of someplace called the Lewis Building? It's an historic mansion in midtown."

"Oh yeah. I think I went there once as a kid for a school trip. Those mannequins kind of creeped me out."

"No kidding... Well, something big might be happening there. I'm going to get in contact with the owner, find out what their security situation is. I need you to do some research about its history, maybe get a layout of the building, anything else that might help."

"You got it, boss."

"I'll check back with you later," I said, leaving him to his task. "I need to make a few phone calls."

I was exhausted by the time the girl left. Not from any physical exertion, but rather the mental energy I had to expend while we waited for the detective to arrive. I could feel the old woman continuously probing at us with her prying eyes, and while I tried not to show it, it took a great deal of focus to resist her gaze. Thankfully, once I let the girl go, the prying eyes went with her. She had looked relieved to be going home. The irony was likely lost on her that she was actually safer with me.

Sadly, my nap was not very rejuvenating. Though I fell asleep quite as suddenly as I laid down, I was haunted by strange and unsettling dreams, more so even than usual. The girl was there, sitting beside me in a crowded auditorium. She introduced herself to me, but I don't recall hearing her say Vivian. I was her age, and rather nervous. I was fumbling haplessly for some charming words to say to her, and finding none. Then all of a sudden, we were up on a stage before the crowd, and she was using some powerful magic to try to kill me while the people cheered her on. From behind the curtains, malevolent eyes stared coldly at us. I pleaded with her. I didn't understand why we were fighting. I desperately wanted to stop. She looked down at me with fire in her eyes, her face twisted up with hatred and disgust, and shouted an incantation. I could feel my lungs burning.

I awoke quite suddenly, and was unsure at first whether I was still dreaming, as I fumbled in the darkness and gasped for air that would not come. I was vulnerable while I slept, and so there was nothing stopping the old woman from tormenting me further. I did not react with much grace under pressure, but this was fairly justified by my reckoning. Whether you are an ordinary human being or a powerful mage, awakening suddenly to one's bed trying to crush you to death is an unsettling experience. I reasoned that some amount of screaming and flailing was called for.

While the animated mattress was not strong enough to crush me outright, death by smothering remained a distinct possibility, as I was unable to pry myself free. My attempts to escape into the æther were being countered by the old crone as well, leaving me trapped. I struggled to push the writhing mass away from my face at least, but without success. The beast would not relent, and I was running out of air.

Not wanting to lose my head and thus probably my life, I took a figurative deep breath and considered my options. I could trying resist her spying spell just as before and then escape, but that would take time and every second brought me closer to unconsciousness. If nothing else, I could use another Interrupt, but I didn't like the thought of losing my magic for even longer than before. Speaking the word aloud might prove too difficult anyway. And really, it shouldn't require such a dire move to escape something as mundane as an enchanted piece of furniture. Surely I knew a spell that could dispel enchantments quickly. I was certain I knew it by name, perhaps even used it sometime recently. I tried frantically to recall the name associated with the effect. Disenchant? Dispel? Dismiss? Yes, that was it.

    Dimitto.

The mattress at once unfurled and flopped lifelessly back onto the floor. I lied splayed out in a sweaty heap atop what was very nearly my death bed. I glared up at the old woman's remote presence and focused on resisting her. After a few moments, I felt her third eye shut. I took a few deep labored breaths, picked up my hat off of the floor where it had tumbled, then shifted to æthereal form and took to the sky with some urgency.

Prior to that moment, I had no intention of ever interacting with the old woman and her group again. Since I had no desire to share their secrets, I thought she would eventually realize this and give up trying to follow me. Instead, she had attempted to kill me while I slept. Worse, she crushed my favorite hat. I stopped briefly on a random rooftop to fix it, and while I managed to bend it back into shape, there were noticeable creases left across the top. Even if no one else noticed, I would know they were there, and that was all that mattered anyway. My only choice was retaliation.

The old woman made further attempts to spy on me as I traveled, but I was sufficiently prepared to prevent them by then. In my free moments, I decided to skim through my notebook for ideas. Most of its contents were of no help to my current situation, but I knew somewhere within was a reference to a spell I had all but forgotten about until recently. Eventually I found the page in question. I hadn't used the spell in a long time; my past self advised it be used "for emergencies". As far as I was concerned, tangling with this particular group qualified as a possible emergency. I noted the warning and set about attempting to familiarize myself with the spell again. I recalled there was a specific hand gesture involved in its casting. I'm not sure if this was originally meant to confuse someone trying to learn the spell, to permit more complex target selection, or simply for my own amusement. In any case, the gesture was simple enough to recall, muscle memory being the more reliable type of memory in most cases. However, going through the motions left my heart feeling inexplicably heavy. I tried not to ponder on the matter any further.

As the sun began to set, I approached the museum to face the madam. The building was closed when I arrived; all the better for a one-on-one meeting. I slipped inside through the second story wall and set my feet on the floor, shifting back to my physical body as I did so. No one came out to meet me at first. I wandered the halls for some minutes, thumbing idly through my notebook.

"Wait as long as you like," I said, trusting I would be heard. "I'm not leaving until you come out and face me."

Finally, a door opened down the hall. Out stepped a portly man in a dusty jacket with a top hat and monocle. I vaguely remembered him from the last time I visited. I turned to face him.

"You have returned!" He sneered. "Loathsome whelp! I beseeched our beloved Madam Hortence not to entrust a mere girl with your capture. But no matter, for now I shall dispatch you myself, once and for all!"

I rolled my eyes and put the notebook away.

"Will you please stop that? This fau-ristocrat routine of yours fools no one. Nobody in Victorian times, or any other time for that matter, has ever talked that way. I'm amazed it worked on the girl, even with the old woman's charm on her."

Another door opened at the opposite end of the hall behind me.

"You'll have to forgive Mister Harold. He has a great flair for the dramatic."

I turned to face the new voice, and out stepped another Victorian-looking gentleman, taller with a more muscular frame, with glasses resting on the bridge of his nose. I was fairly certain these two were the ones who tried to take me against my will the last time I visited.

"Though if I'm not mistaken," he continued, "you seem to be putting on airs to some degree as well."

I shrugged. "I'm an eccentric. We're allowed to speak in meandering gibberish if it pleases us."

"It's still not too late, you know. You could make a fine addition to our society, if only you would set aside your ego and learn to live in peace with us."

"You tried to have me eaten by a mattress. We're several miles past putting our differences aside at this point. I came to put the old Red Queen in her place, but if she won't show herself, I'll gladly settle for Tweedle-Dee and Tweedle-Dum in the interim. Feel free to decide amongst yourselves who is who."

"You insolent fool!" the portly one growled. "Come, Sir Calvin! Let us rid our home of this pest!"

"Gladly."

The tall one held out his hand, and a glowing ball of flames materialized in his palm. Grinning, he launched the fireball toward me. It grew larger and roared louder as it flew down the hall, drawing closer. The roaring flames soon filled the hallway and became a moving wall of fire. I stifled a laugh as it bore down on me, then glanced over my shoulder to see the round one casting the same knockout bolt spell they'd given to the girl before. I flicked my wrist in his direction, countering his bolt before it could reach me, then pointed and fired a bolt of my own at the tall one as the fire engulfed me.

The old woman was definitely watching by this point, ready to counter any attempt I made to escape through the æther. Not that I needed to. The fire was an obvious distraction, a red herring to give the round one a chance to try a knockout spell while my back was turned. While it looked convincing enough, there was no part of me that believed these buffoons possessed a fire spell as potent as what I was seeing.

Even if they did, there was no way they would cast it in their own home and burn the place to the ground in the process. And even on the remote chance they were just that reckless and inept, the room didn't feel any hotter with the fire's appearance.

I had plenty of time to consider all of these things in the second or so it took the large one to react to the illusion and attack me. I was accustomed to facing much keener minds and faster reflexes in a duel, and Vivian had given me a welcome opportunity to shake off whatever rust had accumulated after many decades being out of practice. The temperamental twosome offered me plenty of microseconds to spare, which I obligingly spent considering the nature of caterpillars. Funny little things, aren't they? So squat and squishy, yet so full of potential to soar with beauty and grace. There's likely a fine poetic metaphor in there somewhere, but I let the thought go unexplored. I was still technically in a fight for my life, so it would do me well to pay attention.

The brilliant flames passed over me harmlessly, as expected. The portly gentleman had waited to see whether his bolt would strike true before preparing any more; also expected. What I did not expect was for my own knockout bolt to pass just as harmlessly through the tall man. He grinned mockingly at me, completely unaffected.

"A good try, adept," he quipped, "but not good enough."

I shook my head. What had just happened didn't make any sense. He didn't counter the spell, and he didn't resist it. The bolt went right through him as if he wasn't even there. He couldn't just be another illusion; illusory images can't cast their own spells that way, and I most definitely saw him summoning the fireball. I could detect some unfamiliar magic enchantment around him, but nothing that resembled any illusion. There had to be another reason the spell had no effect. As he laughed at me, I stood dumbfounded for a few long seconds before the reason dawned on me.

"Oh, for the love of..."

The tall one chuckled. "As if you could ever hope to defeat us with such rudimentary magic. If that is all you came prepared with, this is going to end poorly for you."

"And painfully, I would add!" the round one chimed in.

I glared hard at the tall one, and began marching toward him.

"You have no chance to win this," he said. "Just

give up now and perhaps we'll be merciful."

"So stupid..." I muttered to myself, shaking my head. "How did I not see it?"

I kept walking toward him at a steady pace. He took a step back.

"That's far enough."

He fired a knockout bolt at me, and the round one launched another of his own from behind. I easily countered both and continued walking.

"Don't you understand?" the tall one demanded. I was only a few steps away and closing, but he held his ground. "Nothing you can do, no spell you can cast will harm us. We are immortal! You have no hope of defeating us! And now that you have insulted us, you will never-"

I reared back and punched him straight in the jaw as hard as I could. His head flew off of his shoulders and tumbled across the carpet. His body crumpled to the floor with a hollow plastic clatter; the enchantment that had been animating it had collapsed as well. I shook my head again and kicked the torso, scattering the remaining pieces of the mannequin across the hall.

"How did I not realize sooner? Ugh..."

"W-what?! What have you done?!"

The round one wailed as I turned toward him

and began walking back in his direction.

"Come on out and show yourself now," I said, the annoyance in my tone ringing clear as a bell. "I'm getting tired of playing with your toys."

"*Adripio!*"

The round one shouted and thrust his hand toward me. A flurry of brightly glowing magical bolts shot out in quick succession. They were still clearly the same base spell, just being cast rapid-fire. I held out my hand and countered all of them, my wrist flicking back and forth as I mentally adjusted my focus to each bolt in turn until they were all gone.

"Thanks for announcing the spell just in case I didn't already recognize it. It certainly makes countering much easier. Is that the only real dueling spell you know? Honestly, and you tried to accuse *me* of coming unprepared..."

"You think you have won, adept?!" the round man roared, having yet to realize I'd already won. "I have restrained myself thus far in order to avoid making a horrific mess in our beautiful hallway. But now I can see you have left me no choice! The time has come to unleash the full brunt of my awesome power upon you! For I..."

As his voice rambled on, I closed one eye and held out my hand in front of me, my index finger and thumb framing his face in my perspective. His tirade stopped prematurely.

"W-what is that you are doing?" he asked.

"I'm crushing your head."

"I beg your pardon?"

My fingers closed together, pinching the space between my fingertips. The effect only took a fraction of a second. A deafening crack echoed through the building like a peal of thunder. My heart skipped a beat, and my eardrums ached. I had forgotten about the alarming side-effect of this spell on the surrounding air pressure. Furniture trembled, and framed pictures clattered against the walls. The portly mannequin's head and upper body were gone, ripped violently away from their state of physical existence. The rest fell into a pile of broken plastic and torn fabric.

I held my hand over my chest, hoping to calm the frantic pounding that had just started within. I looked around, still sensing the old woman's presence. If I didn't have her attention before, I certainly did then. I caught my breath before speaking.

"That was a warning. Stay away from me. Don't follow me, don't watch me, don't ever bother me again. Otherwise, if you really are immortal, I'll make you wish you could die."

I shifted back to æthereal form and flew away from that place. She made no effort to stop me.

Chapter 15: Normalcy

I hadn't made much progress by Sunday morning. I spent most of the previous night too worried about Vivian to focus much on research. I left a message with her and her parents to call me directly if they had any problems. Still, I couldn't help worrying she might be attacked again while I was away. I was tempted to use *Aspicio* again, but since the Chief didn't want me discussing magic unless it was in person, I couldn't tell her about the spell yet and thus couldn't get her permission to use it. Without that permission, I'd be crossing a serious legal and ethical boundary. If I chose to ignore that boundary, even if I had good intentions, I didn't like what that might say about me as a person.

James got some information on the Lewis Building's history and current ownership, but nothing that wasn't publicly available. I kept getting the building manager's voicemail when I called. I tried calling Vivian again that morning and similarly got no response. Remembering what it was like to be a teenager, I decided she was probably sleeping in and just left her a message saying to call me back when she was ready to talk more. My last call that morning was a personal one rather than professional. I confirmed my weekly brunch with my mom.

I always took a break on Sunday mornings to spend some time with her. Since I moved out and got a job, she's been all alone in her little apartment, so I feel a bit guilty if I don't see her regularly. She's probably fine, but I still like seeing her anyway, catching up and talking about how work is going. Plus, she really makes the best omelets.

"A promotion! That's just wonderful." She praised me as we ate. "Of course, I always knew you were going places. You're such a smart, hard-working young man. It's just great you have a boss that already appreciates that. You know when I started at my job I didn't see a penny of a raise for a whole three years. Can you believe that? Anyway, good for you John."

"Thanks. It's not a lot, but it's nice to be recognized I guess."

"M-hm. I'm just so happy for you, sweetheart. I wish I could get a little recognition at work. Especially when... well, never mind, I don't want to spoil the mood."

"What is it, Mom?"

We've been through this before. Her tired eyes wandered away, avoiding mine.

"Oh, it's nothing. It's just that my hours got cut again at work, and with the rent almost due-"

"It's fine, Mom. I'll take care of it."

"Sweetie, you don't have to. Really, I'm fine. I was just thinking aloud."

"Mom, I said it's fine. I want to help."

I don't know why she makes me drag it out of her every time. I don't mind lending her money, but she never wants to just come out and ask directly. Maybe she's a little ashamed to be making less than I do, like it's her job as the mother to keep providing.

"Thank you. I promise, I'll pay you back when I can."

"I know, Mom. You know you're good for it. We're family."

She smiled and shook her head, then looked down at my folder sitting on the table.

"So what's this? You're starting to bring your work home with you?"

I shrugged. "I guess. Things are getting sort of busy at the station right now. I spent so much time focusing on this one case, and then... Well, I can't go into details, obviously. Ongoing investigations and all."

"I know, I understand. Don't get yourself in trouble on my account."

I glanced at the clock on the wall. It was going

on noon.

"I should probably get going in a few minutes," I said. "Want some help with the dishes?"

"I've got them, sweetie. You do enough for me as it is."

"Alright. I'm just going to hit the bathroom quick."

I got up and headed to the bathroom. As I was washing up afterward, I felt a buzz in my pocket. I dried my hands and took out my phone. There was a text message from Vivian.

"*help plz*"

The brevity and word choice had me very concerned. Deciding I no longer had a choice, I closed my eyes and focused.

Aspicio Vivian.

I almost gasped when the image appeared in my mind. Instead of Vivian, I was looking at the ghost. He seemed to be looking back at me, a disapproving scowl on his face. I only saw it for a split second, then the image suddenly went black, and my eyes snapped open again.

I rushed out of the bathroom, barely looking up from my phone as I sped past my mom and toward the door.

"Something came up," I called back as I got my

coat on. "I really gotta run. Sorry. Love you."

"Oh, um, okay. Love you, too."

I clambered down the stairs, barely watching my step as I tried to call Vivian's number on my phone. I held it to my ear as I headed for the parking lot. She wasn't answering. I tried dialing again as I pulled out of the parking lot, and still no response.

"Dammit. Vivian, please be okay..."

My parents let me sleep in nice and late Sunday morning. Usually they don't like me rolling out of bed close to noon, even if it's on weekends. I've tried several times to explain to them that college students are the most sleep-deprived people on Earth and that weekends are prime time to catch some extra Z's to make up for the late nights (studying of course), but they won't hear it. This time was a little different though. After the whole kidnapping thing, I was pretty sure I had earned a chance to sleep in, and maybe even be treated to some chocolate-chip pancakes when I got up.

After I got out of the shower, I checked my phone and found I had two new voicemails waiting, which was strange for a Sunday morning. Also, I didn't think anyone even used voicemail anymore. I always assumed it was just there for old people who had arthritis, or were just too techno-phobic to learn how texting works. I played the first message and listened as I got dressed.

"*Hi, Vivian. This is Detective Powers. Just wanted to give you an update. I've been bringing my superior up to speed on what we talked about. It sounds like he's really on board, but I think we need a more concrete view of the situation before we can go any further. If there are any more specifics you can tell us, I think they would be a big help. Let me know when you're available to come by the station and talk. The sooner the better. I'll call back later to confirm. Thanks."*

I had spent a good chunk of Saturday night thinking of how to confront Madam Hortence. Even with John helping me, I didn't like our chances much. Maybe we needed a different strategy. I played the second message.

"Hey Viv, this is your Uncle Jim. Hope you're doing okay. I heard from your mom you had kind of a scary night. I'm glad you didn't get hurt. No big surprise there, I guess. I always tell people you're a lot tougher than you look. Ah, anyway, sorry to bother you at a time like this, but I wanted to check that you still have your key to the building. We had a problem with some vandals, last night I think. I came in to open up this morning and found two of the mannequins torn to pieces in the middle of the hallway-"

I lost my balance and almost fell on my face while trying to put my jeans on. My phone clattered to the floor. I quickly snatched it up and brought it close to my ear.

"...*a million years think that you would do something like this, or let any of your friends in after dark or anything. I just have to ask because I couldn't find any sign somebody broke in, and aside from me you're the only one with a key to get in. Maybe you dropped it or something, I don't know. I just don't want you getting in trouble over it if you were involved somehow, so I'm putting off talking to the police as long as I can, but you gotta get back to me, Viv. If you know anything about this let me know, okay? Alright. Stay outta trouble, kiddo.*"

Once I was fully dressed, I called Uncle Jim back. I tried to sound clueless, even though I had a pretty good idea who was responsible. The two mannequins he described sounded just like Sir Calvin and Mister Harold. I let him know I still had my key and didn't let anybody in. At least I could be honest about that. I offered to stop by and help clean up, but he said not to worry about it, and he'd let me know when he finds out more. I thanked him and hung up as I felt my heart starting to race.

I thought Sir Calvin used his magic to disguise himself and the others as mannequins. It never occurred to me any of them could have actually been mannequins all along. I knew Mister Harold could animate objects to make them move on their own, and they could even seem pretty lifelike sometimes, but if he was just a puppet himself, then who animated him? How many of these people were even real?

"Vivian, honey, are you up yet?" Mom's voice broke my train of thought.

"Uh, yeah, I'm coming."

I started toward the stairs and found her already waiting at the bottom.

"Honey, there's another detective here asking to talk to you. If you're not feeling up to it, I could ask him to come back another time."

"Oh no, I'm fine. Hang on."

As I walked down the stairs and rounded the corner, I could hear Dad in the front room talking to him.

"Here she comes now."

Dad smiled and gave me a little wave as I approached, then turned back toward the couch.

"You know, I can't believe how well she's taking it," he continued. "My wife and I have just been beside ourselves. To think someone would just take an innocent girl hostage and threaten her life to try to evade the police. What kind of sick person does something like that?"

"There are some real monsters out there, sir."

I entered the room, and stopped dead in my tracks when I saw the 'detective' sitting there, wearing a black overcoat and his usual black bowler hat. He looked up and shot me a sly smile. For my family's sake, I tried not to look panicked.

"What do you want?" I demanded.

Dad furrowed his brow. "Vivian, there's no need to be rude-"

"It's alright, sir. I can imagine how she must be feeling right now."

The guy in the bowler hat stared hard into my eyes. I tried not to look nervous.

"Vivian, I just want to talk for a minute, and then I'll be out of your hair. I promise."

His mouth stopped moving, but I still heard his voice in my head. *You don't want them to know about me. Neither do I. Let's not make this difficult.*

"Okay."

I nodded. I could make this work to my advantage. Whatever he wanted to know, I was going to get some answers of my own first.

"We can talk outside," I said.

"That's fine. I shouldn't stay long anyway." He stood up and gestured to the front door. "After you."

I walked out onto the front porch and down the steps, the guy following a few paces behind me. I tried to subtly sneak my phone out of my pocket, put it on silent mode, and discretely fired off a text to John before slipping the phone back into my front pocket as I walked down the driveway. There wasn't anyone else on our street at the moment, so the driveway would be private enough for our conversation. I glanced back to make sure my parents weren't watching.

"Before I tell you anything," I said, glaring at him, "what happened at the Lewis Building last night?"

"You tell me. I thought there was a group of mages living there, and instead I was confronted by a couple of animated toys. So were you lying to me?"

"No! I thought they were all real people. Hey, they fooled you, so how could you expect me to know better?"

"You've spent a great deal more time around them than I have. Months, from what you told me. How could you not notice something amiss?"

"Uh, illusions and mind-control magic. Duh."

He crossed his arms. "Alright, there's no need to get snippy about it."

"Why did you go back in the first place? I thought you said you were done with them."

"My bed tried to eat me; it was her doing, if that wasn't clear. I got fed up with the old bat pestering me so I went to send a message: leave me alone. I haven't heard a reply so I can only assume it was received."

"So, how many of them are even real?"

"I'm not positive, but the more I think about it, the more likely it seems that it's just one person. One lonely fool using magic to create their own little fantasy land in that old building. It's essentially the world's biggest doll house."

Looking at it that way, a part of me almost felt sorry for Madam Hortence. Then I remembered how she tried to kill me, and the pity faded quickly.

"I guess it's possible. So, how did you figure out they were mannequins?"

"One of them was immune to a spell that only affects living..." He furrowed is brow. "When did this turn into *you* interrogating *me*?"

I gave an innocent shrug. He rolled his eyes.

"You're lucky I like you. Now, are you going to answer my question?"

"If I can. What is it?"

"Do you think she really is immortal?"

I wasn't sure how to answer that. As long as I'd known about Madam Hortence and her people, I had taken her at her word that they were immortal mages that had been around since Victorian times, if not earlier. But my judgment wasn't so clear back then.

Now that he posed the question, I found I had serious doubts.

"I'm not sure. Does it matter?"

"I wouldn't have asked otherwise."

"Honestly, I don't know. Do *you* think she is?"

He sighed. "I was skeptical about her claimed immortality from the start, considering some of her awkward speech patterns, and the apparent gaps in her knowledge. But then I found out she had created herself a group of imaginary friends. That does seem like the kind of thing an immortal would do. It also adds a clearer motivation to her choice to bring you into that circle. Whether you wound up being used as her pawn or not, initially she may have just wanted someone new to talk to. That's still not enough to prove anything though. I need to be certain."

"How can I tell if someone is immortal?"

"It would hardly be obvious, but it should become clearer once you have gotten to know them. Did she ever talk about her past life, for example? Any past acquaintances?"

"Not really. She talked a bit about how they came over from England in the mid-eighteen-hundreds, and they secretly moved into the Lewis Building, which was empty after the original family had vacated. She was pretty vague with the details."

"Is there any physical evidence of her existing in the past? That building has a lot of old paintings and photographs on the walls. Does she appear in any of them?"

"No..." Another detail I wish I'd noticed earlier. "I've looked at every picture in there and she's never appeared in one. I guess if she didn't want to be found, that would make sense..."

I started pacing around a bit as I thought aloud.

"Something doesn't add up though. I would think she'd have to interact with other owners at some point, but the way she told it they just moved in and had been living there in secret ever since. I'm supposedly the first person she talked to in over a hundred years. How could she go all that time without being discovered? She couldn't have just been doing the mannequin routine that whole time; the building wasn't opened to the public as a historic site until the late 20ᵗʰ century."

Just then another important detail hit me.

"Oh god, the fire. I almost forgot about that. Huge portions of the Lewis Building had to be restored in 1909 after a fire nearly burnt it to the ground. It would have been totally uninhabitable for about two years. She never once mentioned having to leave after they initially moved in. At the time I thought she was just glossing over it..."

He shook his head. "She was lying. Either she didn't know about the fire, or it didn't fit into her fantasy. Figures."

He cast his eyes down at the sidewalk. I was a little taken aback.

"You... wanted her to be immortal?"

"Maybe. It doesn't really matter now."

I had assumed he wanted to know if she was immortal to better gauge how dangerous she might be. His disappointment had to mean there was more to it. I wasn't sure what his reasons were, but it was clear he didn't want to tell me. I had a more important angle to work anyway.

"Well hey, look on the bright side. This probably means she's not nearly as powerful as we first thought. Taking her down should be no problem at all."

He raised an eyebrow. "Taking her down?"

"Look, she tried to kill you, right? And she tried to kill me. We've got a common enemy here. We should be working together to stop her."

He sighed and covered his face with his palm. "Let's ignore for a moment the fact that when you say 'working together', you mean 'having me do your dirty work for you.' What you've failed to account for is that at this point, I don't *want* to stop her. She isn't my problem anymore, she's just yours. If you want help getting rid of her, why don't you ask your detective friend?"

"I did, and if I'm lucky he's still going to help me, but this would be so much easier for somebody like you."

He shook his head, and I scowled.

"You think I like having to ask for help with this? I hate it. *I* should be the one using magic to take down Madam Hortence. Instead I have to try and plead with a selfish creep, or beg a rookie cop who's obsessed with catching the selfish creep. Magic is wasted on you guys. It's so stupid. Why don't *I* get to have the special magical blood or whatever? Why can't it be me?"

As I voiced my frustration, he started looking off into the distance past me. It wasn't his usual lost-in-thought look, though. He actually seemed to be staring at something. I almost turned around to look when he stopped.

"Er, pardon me. I wasn't ignoring you. Someone keeps trying to eavesdrop on our conversation. Maybe multiple someones."

He looked around us a bit longer, then turned back to me again.

"Believe it or not, I agree with you," he said, to

my amazement. "It isn't right at all, a few 'special' people being given access to magic and the rest of the world left powerless. It wasn't meant to be like this..."

Then he started getting that distant look from before. This one seemed to last longer, but stopped abruptly when his eye twitched. He held a hand up over his face and shook his head. I couldn't think of anything to say at that point. I took the opportunity to sneak a peek at my phone; the screen was lit up showing an incoming call. The guy took his little notebook out from his pocket and started absently thumbing through it.

"You may as well answer that. I think we're done here."

He started walking away, eyes buried in that notebook. I waited a second to make sure he was gone before checking my phone again. It was John's number.

"Hello?" I answered.

"*There you are. Are you okay? I tried to check on you a minute ago and I saw-*"

"The guy with the hat."

"*Yes! What's happening there? Is he with you?*"

"He just left. And I'm fine, but I think we need to talk. 'The sooner the better'."

"*Agreed. I'm on my way over now to get you.*

Just sit tight for a few minutes, okay?"

"Okay. See you in a few."

"Thanks. Bye."

I ended the call and walked back up to the house. Mom was waiting near the door.

"Hey," I said, "so the detective from yesterday wants to talk more. He's going to give me a ride to the station in a few minutes. Is that okay?"

"More questions?" She shook her head. "I don't understand why they need to keep bothering you like this, especially so soon after a traumatic experience."

"I'm fine, Mom. And I'm a really credible eyewitness. You know how rare those are?"

"They want her help, let her help," Dad chimed in from the kitchen. "The sooner that bastard is behind bars, the sooner we can all sleep more soundly."

"Alright," Mom conceded. "Just make them promise to have you home before dinner."

I rolled my eyes. "I will. Thanks, Mom."

I sat and waited on the front porch for just a few minutes. John came around the corner and parked in front of my house. He waved me toward the car, and I got up and started down the front walk. As I walked, he took a sip from his travel mug. I was a little puzzled as he kept staring at it right up until I got to the car and opened the door. He didn't break his concentration until we both heard a shout from the porch.

"Please have her home by six o'clock, officer! Vivian, I'm going to make your favorite tonight!"

"Oh my god, Mom..."

I shook my head and got into the passenger seat of the car.

"What was that about?" John asked.

"Nothing. What were you staring at?"

He set the mug down in the cup holder.

"My mentor has some trick to heat up coffee with magic, and he won't tell me how it works. I've been trying to figure it out."

"So you're trying to cast a spell that you don't know the name of? I don't think that's how spells work."

"Well, would you tell him that? He seemed to think I could work it out. It's probably time you met him anyway. I'll have to check with him first, but he's going to need to be able to trust you if we're going to work together on this."

I buckled in and we started driving.

"So," I asked, "what was that about you checking in on me? I didn't see you anywhere on the street."

"Oh, yeah... So, last night after I talked to you, I learned a new spell that lets me see someone wherever they are just by focusing on them."

"Wow. Sounds like pretty advanced stuff."

"Maybe. It's supposed to let me see anyone I'm familiar with. When I got your message earlier I tried to see what was going on here, but I think my suspect was blocking me out somehow."

"Madam Hortence must have something similar, since her people were able to find me so far from the Lewis Building. If hat-guy knows about it, he could probably resist the effect. Heck, he might even know the exact spell and be able to counter it. He was a real pain to find the first time."

"You don't say..." He shook his head. "Anyway, I got in the car expecting the worst, but you sounded pretty calm on the phone. Everything's really okay?"

"Yeah."

I gave him a recap of my conversation from earlier. He seemed as surprised as I was that the guy had apparently shown up just to talk, and left without incident.

"Well, I suppose this is good news for us," he said. "I'm supposed to focus on dealing with Madam Hortence and her people now. If we have less of them to deal with, or even just one, maybe it'll make this whole thing easier."

I smiled. "Alright. It's about time she got what's coming to her."

"But I'm concerned that my suspect seems to know where you live. Aren't you worried about him too?"

"Kind of, but... I don't get the feeling he wants to hurt me. He had plenty of opportunity when we were all alone and he didn't do anything. I can't see why he would try to now. I kind of worry he's going to try watching me in the shower or something, but between that and the threat on my life, Madam Hortence is definitely the bigger worry for me right now. Although..."

"What?"

"I don't know if this means anything, but... Here's the thing. When he was holding me hostage, before you showed up, we wound up talking for quite a while, long after I told him everything he wanted to know about Madam Hortence's group. He said I reminded him of somebody he knew once, but he wasn't sure how exactly. He asked me about my schoolwork, and what I've been reading for class. At first I thought he was just playing mind games or whatever, but after a while I started to think maybe he's just that lonely.

"Now I could just be reading into things here, but I'm seeing a definite pattern. He wears mismatched anachronistic clothing for whatever reason. He talks like he's seen it all and done it all, and has at least a few skills to back it up. From what I can tell, he doesn't really have anybody else he can talk to in his life, at least not anymore. The conversation we had today about Madam Hortence just reinforces what I was already thinking: what if *he's* actually the one who's immortal? I don't know, does that sound totally crazy?"

He looked surprised. "Actually, that kind of fits with a theory I'm working on now. You should see this picture that James pulled from- Oh, crap."

"What?"

"I just realized, I left my mom's place in such a hurry that I forgot my files. I'll have to show you later."

"You were at your mom's place just now?"

"We have brunch together most Sundays."

He said it so matter-of-factly, I had to chuckle.

"Seriously? I thought one of the perks of becoming an adult was not having your parents around all the time."

"I happen to like seeing her every week. She's a very nice person, and a great cook."

"Uh-huh." I grinned. "'A boy's best friend is his mother', huh?"

He laughed. "Okay, let's ignore the fact that you just compared me to a serial killer. Aren't you like 18? Why are all the references you make from movies that came out before your parents were even born?"

I shrugged. "I like old things."

We went back to the police station, where John introduced me to his boss and gave him an update on the situation. I was thrilled that the chief was so into the idea of us working together and taking down Madam Hortence. He actually suggested that John should go and confront her right away, hopefully catching her off-guard. John seemed uneasy but the chief was confident, saying he'd keep an eye on things from afar with the spying spell and help out however he could. I reminded him I'd be there to help too, which for some reason took both of them by surprise. They tried to talk me out of going along, pointing out how dangerous it could be. Apparently they haven't learned by now that I'm totally unstoppable.

Eventually they relented, and maybe an hour later John and I were walking up to the Lewis Building. Uncle Jim was out front waiting for us.

"Hey, Viv. And Detective Powers, I take it? Right this way."

I had called ahead to let Uncle Jim know a detective would be stopping by to investigate. Luckily he had the foresight to keep the museum closed for the day until the police could come by to check the place out. I was confident we could keep the situation under control, but if not, at least we wouldn't have to worry about innocent bystanders getting hurt. He led us up to the front door and unlocked it for us.

"You really think your suspects could be hiding out in here?" he asked as he unlocked the front door for us.

"It's a distinct possibility," John replied. "I don't know how dangerous they could be, but just in case I think it's best if you wait out here and let me handle this."

"Yes, sir."

John turned to me, and I crossed my arms. He sighed.

"Is there even any point in me telling you to wait here?"

"Probably not," Uncle Jim answered for me. "If there's somebody in there who damaged museum property, they need to be afraid of her, not the other way around."

I smiled sweetly. "Aw. Thanks."

John shook his head, barely hiding a smile. "Fine. But you're staying behind me."

Slowly, we made our way through the foyer and into the main hall. Everything was quiet. We walked cautiously, looking around at all the possible angles someone could approach from. No one was coming out to meet us. I pointed toward a doorway on our right, leading to the parlor. That room usually had two mannequins, or Miss Beatrice and Lord Irving as I had known them, posed there during the day. As we passed through the doorway I saw them in their usual spot, standing facing one another as if having a conversation.

"I'm not feeling anything magical in here," John whispered to me. "How do we know if they're really people or just mannequins?"

I walked over to Beatrice and lifted her up by the shoulders. The top half of her body separated easily from the bottom half. I set the mannequin torso down on the floor.

"Well, that's one way."

John walked up to Irving and did the same as I'd done. He seemed surprised how light the mannequin body was. It slipped out of his grip momentarily and he awkwardly lunged forward and caught it, though not before the gentleman's outstretched arm bounced against the floor with a soft plastic smack.

"Sorry," he said, setting the mannequin down gently.

"Most of them would usually be upstairs. Let's go."

We exited the room, continued to the stairs and up to the second floor. I pointed toward the gallery. John opened the left door slowly and peered inside, then waved for me to follow as he stepped through. Four other mannequins were arranged around the table, posed to depict them sharing a meal. I noticed the seat at the head of the table was conspicuously empty.

"Madam Hortence isn't here. She'll probably be in the study-"

The door slammed shut behind us. The people around the table slowly turned to us, glaring angrily. John's face wrinkled up, and he inhaled sharply like he was in pain as the group rose to their feet. He gestured for me to stay behind him, as if I needed an invitation.

"You remember what to do if they try a knockout spell, right?" I asked him. I had explained the basics of dueling as best I could on the car ride over.

"In theory. I've never countered a spell before, let alone four at once."

The nearest gentleman raised his hand as if preparing to cast a spell, then suddenly leaned forward and toppled to the floor. His plastic head bounced off of his shoulders and tumbled toward us. The others looked on in surprise, and one by one their shocked faces changed back to lifeless masks, and they all collapsed to the floor as well.

"What just..." Before I finished my question, I realized what had happened, as did John.

"Thanks, Chief," he said, looking up. "So, how many does that leave?"

"Just her. Come on, let's finish this."

I opened the door and we stepped back out into the hallway. To our left, the door to the study slowly swung open. We walked cautiously toward it, John staying just a few steps ahead of me. I could feel my heart pounding as we inched closer.

"She's probably going to try to charm you," I said. "If you start to feel funny in any way, don't hesitate to use a dispel on yourself. Or on me for that matter."

"Got it." He nodded, but looked uneasy. "I can't feel the chief watching us anymore. Could she be blocking him out?"

"I guess so. Don't worry, we can handle her."

We walked through the doorway and into the study. Madam Hortence was sitting behind the desk, smiling at us as we walked in. She gestured for us to sit down. My vision started to get a little fuzzy at that point. I could actually feel my body moving toward one of the chairs on its own, but then John's hand on my shoulder stopped me. My mind instantly felt clearer, and I stepped back beside him.

"You're a difficult young man to charm, aren't you?"

She looked up at him placidly, then turned her gaze to me, her smile never waning.

"Vivian, my dear, I'm surprised at you. After all that I've done for you, inviting you into my home and teaching you about magic, you choose to repay my kindness by betraying my trust? How could you?"

"How could *I*?" I almost spat at her. "You put a curse on me! You call that kindness?"

"It was for the greater good, dear, you must understand. I couldn't allow the secret of eternal life to be revealed to the outside world. Our family has lived here in peace for over one hundred years-"

"Just stop it! We already know you're lying. There's no family here. It's just you and a bunch of dolls that you make act like people. And you're not immortal. You haven't been living here since the 1800s. It's all a big lie!"

"Vivian..."

"Madam Hortence," John interrupted, showing

her his badge. "I'm placing you under arrest, for attempted murder. I'm going to need you to come with me back to the station. I would appreciate it if we could do this peacefully."

"This isn't right." She shook her head. Her voice actually seemed to crack. "T-this is my home."

"Please, let's not make this difficult."

"This isn't fun anymore. Stop it."

Her voice was the most noticeably upset I'd ever heard, but her Mona Lisa smile still wouldn't change. Maybe it couldn't.

"It's over," I said. "You lost, okay?"

"No! It's all your fault! You ruined everything!"

She raised her hands, and the contents of the desk flew off in all directions. I narrowly ducked under a fountain pen that almost stabbed me in the head. The desk itself shifted and slowly turned as if its wooden frame were made of muscle, its legs twisting and bending back, and it lumbered menacingly toward us like a headless bull. John stepped into its path to protect me, and it tackled him and pushed him back into the wall, trying to crush him. He laid his hands on it, and slowly the desk creature grew stiff and lurched to a stop, its features twisting back into an ordinary desk.

"It's not fair!" Madam Hortence shrieked. "We

were having fun! Why did you have to ruin it?!"

The bookshelves behind her jumped at her shrill cries, and books began flying off the shelves. I ducked down behind John as he quickly pushed the desk away from the wall, and we both took cover on the floor behind it. Heavy leather-bound volumes hurled themselves at us, thumping loudly against the desk just over our heads. Some of the books continued pursuing us after they hit the floor, flipping open and creeping awkwardly toward us like enormous inchworms. John quickly grabbed and dispelled the ones that got too close.

In the corner of the room, a globe started spinning wildly. It popped off of its axis and began bouncing toward us. I managed to catch it out of midair and quickly passed it to him. I wasn't sure anymore if the situation was more scary or comical. I still didn't have my answer when I peeked around the side of the desk and saw Madam Hortence's chair galloping toward me like a frenzied deer. I yelped and retreated back behind the desk as the chair skidded across the hardwood floor, then tumbled past us end over end and crashed into the wall. It scrambled back to its feet, turned and charged at us again. John blocked it with his foot as it lunged for us, then grabbed the chair by its back and held it down until it became inanimate again.

Behind us, Madam Hortence was screaming and crying incoherently. The floor shook from the bookshelves jumping and tossing restlessly back and forth, their thumping and clattering growing louder. Suddenly, there was a terrible crash, and the whole room fell deathly silent.

We both looked back and saw the bookcases had finally fallen completely over. Madam Hortence had been right in their path. I turned away, not wanting to see what had become of her. John slowly stood up and took a few steps closer.

"Vivian... you need to see this."

Reluctantly, I looked back again, expecting to see blood pooling on the rug. There was no blood. I stood up, and John started picking through the mess. As I watched, he pulled the remains of an arm out from under the collapsed bookshelves. It was just a hunk of plastic, half-crushed with a big crack down the middle.

"No way."

I pulled myself to my feet, and took a few steps closer to be sure of what I was seeing. He dropped the arm on the floor.

"They were all mannequins," he said. "Every single one of them."

"How could..."

I leaned against the desk and started sinking back down to the floor as the truth hit me.

"Oh my god. That spying spell. Whoever created these things was never even here. They just watched and controlled all the mannequins from somewhere else." I shook my head. "The world's biggest doll house..."

John walked over and offered me a hand to help me up to my feet. I didn't take it.

"Maybe we should get you home," he said.

I shot up to my feet and scowled at him. "Seriously?! That's how we're going to end this?"

"I know this isn't the big take-down-the-bad-guys moment you were hoping for, but I don't think there's anything more we can do here."

"Are you kidding? The person who created these things, who tried to kill me, is still out there somewhere. We need to find them!"

"And we've got nothing to go on. They could be just about anywhere, and any-*one*. I wouldn't even know where to start."

I wanted to keep arguing with him, no matter how much sense he was making, but I knew I'd be wasting my breath. I hung my head and bit my lip.

"I'm not saying this case is over," he went on.

"The trail's just gone cold. We're going to need a new lead to pick it up again. But for today, I think this is as far as we're going to get."

"Yeah, I guess so."

I looked around at the terrible mess, books and furniture and things strewn all over the place. All of them were antiques that had been around since long before I was born, some irreplaceable. Most of the books were long out of print, and there they laid with spines broken and pages torn. It seemed like such a senseless waste. The fact that the person responsible for the destruction was getting away with it was almost heartbreaking. Someday, I decided, they'll have to answer for all of it.

"I don't know how I'm going to explain this to my uncle. Do you?"

"For now, I'm going to say I'm not at liberty to discuss it. I think I'd better let the chief figure it out. I'm not very good at these cover stories."

"'Honest men make unconvincing liars'..."

I looked around, walked over to the windows and opened one.

"Okay, how about this? We found the suspect and chased him into this room. There was a big fight, the bad guy messed up the furniture and knocked over the bookshelves, and I was so filled with rage by his reckless abuse of antiques that I grabbed him and threw him out the window."

He chuckled. "Well, it's probably more believable than the real story anyway."

"Heck yeah." I struck a superhero pose. "Another villain vanquished by Vivian Vly!"

The chief sent over a few officers to tape off the crime scene and do a preliminary search of the area, not that they were likely to find anything. When I gave him a quick update over the phone, he didn't seem any more optimistic about catching the culprit than I was. I promised to give him the full run-down as soon as I got back to the station. Before that, I dropped off Vivian back at her parents' house. We would need her to give a statement at some point, but I figured for now she just needed some time to process what just happened. Maybe I needed a few minutes myself.

After dropping her off, I took a detour back to my mom's apartment to get the files I'd left with her.

"Mom?"

I knocked on her door before letting myself in. Inside, I found her sitting on the couch in the living area. The TV wasn't on, and she wasn't reading anything. She had a strange melancholy look on her face. Even as she looked up and smiled at me, her smile seemed pensive.

"Mom? Is everything okay?"

"Sit down, John. We need to talk."

Anxiously, I moved to the couch and sat beside

her.

"Mom, what's going on? Did something happen?"

She shook her head, still forcing a smile. "No, sweetheart, there's nothing to worry about. I've just been thinking, and I've decided it's time we had a talk. About me and your father..."

"My father? Where is this coming from all of a sudden?"

I felt a knot in the pit of my stomach at the mere mention of that deadbeat. I could tell whatever Mom had to say was difficult for her, but she still feigned a smile.

"I'm sorry, John. I haven't been totally honest with you. Things with your father and I were... complicated. I didn't want to tell you all of it when you were growing up. I thought it would be simpler if you just never knew him and never wanted to. I was trying to protect you. But you're a grown man now, and I think you deserve... you need to hear the whole story, so you can make your own decision."

Something in her tone caught me off-guard. She sounded sad, but also maybe a little nostalgic. I remained silent and let her continue.

"Your father and I met at a rally I went to with some friends from college. I knew he had to be at least ten years older than us, maybe more, but I thought he was cute. My friends and I tried to get him to buy us liquor." She laughed softly. "Not only did he refuse, he gave us a whole dressing-down about the dangers of underage drinking. I still couldn't tell you if he was joking or not.

"He was a little intimidating at first. Compared to the guys we'd come to the rally with, he seemed so smart and worldly. He made me laugh a few times too, which was a plus. He'd mentioned the name of a local coffee house he liked, and I started hanging out there a lot just hoping to run into him, which I did a few times. It took me about a week of awkwardly flirting and dropping hints before he asked me out.

"Everyone warned me about getting involved with a man so much older, but we took things slow and got to know each other. I would tell him all about my big plans to get into politics and make a difference. He told me about being a professional gambler. He always had some dramatic story about a high-stakes game that almost cost him his rent, but he'd somehow turn it around in the end and put food on the table for a few more weeks. Even back then, I thought his stories sounded too fanciful to be real. But I saw him play a few poker games with strangers and he seemed to always come out ahead, so I believed he could make a living from it.

"Maybe deep down I just wanted to believe in him. We had so much fun talking over dinner, going out dancing, or just taking a stroll through the park. I think we'd been going out close to a year before I saw his apartment. Even longer before we ever fooled around. We'd been seeing each other for almost two years before I got pregnant."

I was stunned. Anytime my mom talked about my father before, it seemed like he had just led her on, taken advantage of her, and then run off when he had to face the consequences. It was very cut-and-dry: he was an older man who should have known better, preying on a naive young woman. I had assumed they only knew each other a few weeks, months at the most.

"Things seemed so perfect back then," she continued. "We were both so happy. The only times it felt strange were whenever I would try to talk about the past, or the future. He didn't like to talk about himself, at least not about anything real. I never met any of his family. He always said he cared more about living in the moment than dwelling on the past. But it was the same when I'd bring up marriage and starting our own family, the idea of us building something together. His eyes would get sort of sad and distant, and he would say he didn't want to talk about the future. He wanted to focus on today. I tried to be patient, even though I couldn't understand it.

"It turned into an argument a few times. I asked him straight-up if he didn't want to marry me, if he was thinking of leaving, or if there was someone else. He swore up and down I was his one and only girl, and I believed him. He said he was sorry, that he was just worried. He'd make excuses, say we didn't have much money, and he wasn't sure he could afford the wedding he thought I deserved, and he worried he wouldn't be able to support our family. He was also worried about my parents being disappointed in me, which I guess I was too. I said none of that mattered to me and we could find a way to get by, but he insisted that we wait. I trusted his judgment so I went along with it, all the time hoping someday soon he would change his mind and say he was ready to settle down.

"Obviously, we hadn't planned on getting pregnant. We tried to be safe, but I guess nothing is foolproof. I was nervous about telling him, knowing how he might react. When I finally gave him the news, the look in his eyes alone broke my heart. He tried to hide what he was feeling, but I could see it. He was absolutely terrified. For one moment, I was terrified too, thinking he might be furious with me, that he might want me to give you up. Instead he just held me close, and said everything was going to be okay, that he was going to take care of us. I went to sleep that night in his arms, praying he was telling the truth, that everything would be okay.

"The next morning I woke up alone, staring at an envelope full of money on the bedside table. I couldn't tell you exactly how much; I stopped counting after I got to ten thousand, and there was still a lot left. I think I would have been less scared and upset if he had just disappeared and didn't leave anything. I stashed the money away under a loose board in the floors, and left it there for weeks. I lied awake at night wondering what to do, terrified who it might belong to, but nobody ever came looking for it. I still felt too guilty to spend any of it, thinking of what he must have done. At least, that was until the next time the bills came in the mail. I was still out of work at the time, and with a baby on the way. I thought, maybe it was okay. If it could help us get by, just to pay the bills until I could go back to work..."

She looked like she might cry, but no tears came. Maybe she had no tears left to shed over him. She turned and looked at me.

"For a long time I hated him. It's not that he

didn't care about us. He cared, I'm sure of it. It's that for as long as I knew him, he was leading some kind of double-life. I don't know what he was involved in, where that money really came from, but his gambling stories couldn't have been any more than colorful lies. Whatever he was really doing, he was risking my safety and the safety of our unborn child, and in the end he decided he'd rather give us up forever than have to face the truth. I think that money was as much to keep me quiet as it was to take care of us.

"I don't really hate him anymore, though. After countless nights of lost sleep, lying awake replaying the events in my mind, wondering how he could have left us behind like that, I finally understood what he really was: a cowardly criminal. He lied about everything to me. I think half the time he was lying to himself, too. That's why he had to leave. He wasn't a good man, and he wouldn't have been a good husband or father. At least he was honest enough with himself to realize that."

I stayed quiet a few more moments, trying to understand. All of this was stunning enough in itself, but there was more to it. Part of me already knew the answer to the question I was about to ask, but I asked it anyway.

"Mom... why are you telling me all this now?"

Sighing, she leaned forward and picked up my folder full of case files off of the coffee table.

"I knew you would be coming back for these. I didn't mean to be nosy, but I couldn't help noticing the photograph."

She opened the folder and handed it to me. The first page still had the black-and-white photo of my suspect paper-clipped to the top.

"Mom..."

"I don't know how you found him, or what he's done. I'm not going to tell you how to do your job, but please listen to a bit of motherly advice: leave this case. Let someone else deal with him. You don't deserve the heartache, and he doesn't deserve to see what a wonderful young man you've become."

As I stared at the photo in front of me, it started wobbling and shaking. It took me a moment to realize it was my hand trembling.

Chapter 19: Conclusions

Detective Powers met with Chief Riley in his office, the former relaying to the latter the events that had transpired that day at the Lewis Building. Riley had already begun writing up a convincing story about a break-in and teenage vandals to cover up the supernatural elements of the stand-off. The detective then brought up his newest revelation, the identity of his father. To say the least, this came as a bit of a shock.

Riley shook his head, looking more disappointed than surprised.

"Powers, I can't begin to understand what you're going through right now. You know you have my sympathy. But my primary concern right now has to be with protecting this city and its people, and the biggest threat we have to deal with right now isn't your father, it's whoever orchestrated that puppet show inside the Lewis Building. That's what I need you working on."

"Are you seriously telling me not to look for him? After everything he's done, the way he's just been toying with me this whole time, you think-"

"Son, believe me, if I were in your shoes I'd

want to chase him down and wring his neck too. But don't let your anger get the better of you here. I need you focused and ready for anything that comes our way. Whoever controlled the mannequins knows we're onto them now. I wanted to ease you into these kinds of investigations slowly, and chasing a serial cat burglar seemed like a good warm-up, but we're wading into deeper waters now and if things go wrong, I'm afraid even I might not be able to help you. I need to know you're up for this."

Powers shifted in his seat. "I know. I won't get reckless, I promise. But I can't just let this bastard off the hook, especially not now. You want me to be focused? If I'm not actively working to find him, I'm just going to be more distracted. I have a chance at some closure here. I can't walk away from that."

Riley sighed and held a hand up to his face.

"You're a detective. If you wanted closure you got into the wrong line of work. There are going to be a lot of cases that never get tied up neatly, and some of them will get very personal, though few will get as personal as this. If I had anybody else I could assign to this unit I'd have them take point right now, but you're all we've got. That's not a knock on your abilities as a detective or as a mage, it's just a fact. But if you can't compartmentalize and keep your feelings out of the job, this isn't going to work. I can't make this any clearer: I either need you putting everything you've got into this Lewis Building case, or I need you to go on paid leave until you think you're ready to let go of this business with your father. So which is it going to be?"

Powers gritted his teeth, and the two stared at each other for a beat.

"Okay. You're right, this case is more important. I promise, I'll devote all my energies to finding our puppet-master before they can hurt anyone else."

"Glad to hear it."

"And during my investigation, if by some coincidence I run across a suspect in another ongoing investigation, I'll be sure to arrest him any way I can."

"Powers..."

"There's no telling where this case could lead, Chief. At this point, the only witnesses we know of who've had dealings with this puppet master are a college girl and a man in a bowler hat. If Vivian can't help me find any new leads, then I may have to follow up with him. Whatever it takes to protect the people of this city, right?"

The chief shook his head, even as half a smirk crept up under one corner of his mustache.

"You're dismissed. Get to work."

"Yes, sir."

Powers left the room, closing the door behind himself. The chief waited a few seconds until he was gone, then leaned back in his chair and sighed.

"Well, I tried."

"If that could be called trying," I said as I revealed myself, standing beside him. "All you're trying is my patience, Riley. This isn't what we agreed to."

He turned his chair slowly toward me. "Look, I stopped circulation of the composite sketches, and the photo James dug up of you hasn't even been sent out. As far as the rest of the force is concerned, you're nobody of interest. So long as you don't do anything to draw attention to yourself, you've got nothing to worry about from my department."

"There's one very notable exception to that statement: your protégé. In fact, to date he's the only one of your men who has been a significant thorn in my side, and you can't seem to control him."

I slipped back into the æther and then reappeared behind him, leaning on the back of his chair.

"In fact, never mind controlling him. It seems you've actually been encouraging him to investigate me while my attention was drawn elsewhere. I'm beginning to think you're the one who told him to follow me in the first place."

He defiantly jerked his chair around and turned to face me again. I sat on his desk, ignoring the minor discomfort of various papers and office supplies.

"Powers found you all on his own, and he had a file on you long before I had any idea he was looking for you. He would've been set on tracking you down no matter what I said. I thought I might as well give the kid some encouragement, help him develop his abilities. It's not like I ever thought he could catch you."

"That's not the point. If you want any more guidance from me in the future, then you need to keep him away from me. He's an inconvenience, a major inconvenience at this point, and I want him gone. And none of this 'paid leave' nonsense, I want him fired."

"He's a model detective, especially on paper. There's no way I could justify firing him without sparking an internal affairs investigation. Besides, I seriously doubt taking his badge would keep him off your case now. He was obsessed with you even before he found out you were his father."

"He respects you. You could have made it clearer-"

"And why in the hell am I finding out about that

little piece of information from him before I hear it from you? If you would've just told me he was your son when this all started, I could have assigned him to another unit, maybe nipped this whole thing in the bud."

I hesitated, averting my gaze. The chief gave a wry smile as he thoughtfully stroked that ridiculous mustache of his.

"You old dog. You had no idea, did you?" he said with a laugh.

"Oh you're enjoying this now, are you? Do you find this sudden injection of family drama into my life amusing?" I rose to my feet, looming over him with a menacing gaze. "If I wanted to kill you right now, what could you possibly do to stop me?"

"I could offer you a drink."

I thought on that a moment, then smiled. "That would work."

The chief got up and walked to a cabinet by the wall, out of which he produced a bottle of single-malt scotch and two glasses.

"I was hoping to save this for a special occasion, but what the hell?"

He poured about two fingers in each glass and handed one to me. I sat in the chair in front of the desk and indulged as he returned to his seat and did the same. I wouldn't call myself an avid drinker, nor did I even particularly like scotch, but I must have let slip to him at some point that I enjoyed this sort of thing from time to time. Even just watching the amber liquid swirl gently as I rolled the glass in my hand gave me sort of a warm nostalgic feeling, echoing the few times in the past which I could recall fondly. It was almost comforting.

"So," I said, still swirling my drink slowly. "Be honest with me. Do I need to worry about him coming after me again? Or can you keep this under control?"

"If you really want to keep him off your back, maybe you could help me figure out who this puppet master is so I can send him in their direction."

"If I knew anything more about them at this point than you do, I'd be happy to tell you. But I don't."

"Doesn't matter, I guess. Either way, I can't see Powers letting go of this, even if it hadn't gotten so personal. He's an idealist; he sees wrong in the world and he wants to set it right. We could really use more young men like him."

"I can't say I agree." I took another drink from my glass.

"In the interest of keeping his focus on the puppet master and off of you, maybe you could answer another question for me."

"Shoot."

"It would've been a lot easier to convince Powers that you weren't worth our attention if all he had on you were petty thefts. After all this time, why would you suddenly start kidnapping?"

"What, the girl? That's simple. I wanted my notebook back. I needed leverage."

"You and I both know you could have easily stolen the notebook back in no time. Whatever abilities he has to interfere with your ghost routine, Powers couldn't keep the notebook on him at all times. So, why kidnap the girl?"

I shrugged and took another drink. "I was angry that he took it, so I wanted to make him sweat a little. I figured a kidnapped girl might light a fire under his seat. It certainly seemed to do the trick."

"So, it had nothing to do with you seeing an innocent girl dying at your feet and knowing you were the only one who could help her before it was too late?"

I raised an eyebrow. "...Are you implying that I might have a virtuous nature? I take offense at that, sir."

The chief set down his glass and leaned forward, resting his elbows on his desk.

"At the risk of causing further offense, I'm going to suggest an alternate solution to your problems with the law. I want to give you a chance to wipe the slate clean, make things right. If you agree to fly straight from here on, I'm willing to offer you a job working with our Special Investigative Unit. We'll need to fabricate a believable identity for you, but you'd be on the payroll, solving crimes the way only people like us can. I'm willing to bet this puppet master isn't the only magical terror out there. We could really use somebody with your knowledge and abilities on our side."

I blinked. "Did you take a few more hits from that bottle when I wasn't looking? Perhaps I should protect you from yourself."

I grabbed the bottle and refilled my own glass, which had just been emptied. I set the bottle back down and took a drink before continuing.

"Really, now. Are you absolutely stark raving mad? Why would I possibly want to put myself through the misery of remaining in close proximity with this vengeful son of mine *and* helping you fools solve crimes? Has someone gone and written the word 'gullible' across my forehead while I was sleeping?"

Riley shrugged. "It's not such a terrible idea, is it? You want the police off your back. More than that, I think a part of you wants to do something worthwhile with your abilities. That's probably why you brought me into the loop about magic in the first place."

I finished my drink, then took the bottle again and helped myself to another.

"Don't you go projecting your righteous do-goodery onto me, Riley. Do you want to know why I told you about magic? To enjoy the look on your face after I shattered your minuscule conceptions of the nature of reality itself. You were, by the way, severely disappointing in that department. It wouldn't kill you to emote once in a while. That stony visage has done nothing to slow the progression of your ever-deepening wrinkles."

He shook his head and gave his signature half-smirk. I set the bottle down and sat back in my seat with the glass.

"And anyway, I thought perhaps if you felt indebted to me then I wouldn't have to twist your arm quite so hard to make you look the other way on my thievery. Catch more flies with honey, and all that nonsense."

"I don't believe that's all there is to it. You want to make things right somehow. If you stop stealing and work with us, I can make what little evidence there is of your old transgressions disappear. You'll be able to start over like new. And if you do enough good out there with us, maybe even your son will find it in his heart to forgive you."

"What the hell makes you think I want his forgiveness? Or yours, for that matter?"

"Maybe you don't. But you sure seem like you want absolution from someone."

I scoffed and took another drink from my glass, my hand a bit more shaky in transit to my mouth than it should have been. The devilish liquid was gradually taking its toll. I wasn't even certain I could still be intoxicated. Clearly I could.

"I've seen what you're capable of," Riley continued. "You're obviously unstoppable as a thief. You could take anything in this world you desired and get away with it. So that begs the question: why stick to petty crime?"

"I am a man of simple tastes. Besides, it's easier to go unnoticed that way."

"I don't believe you."

He gestured to some files on his desk, only slightly wrinkled from my having sat on them minutes earlier.

"I've been studying what Powers has collected on you, and I think I'm starting to get a clearer picture. You never steal more than a little cash and enough food to scrape by on. You've been caught squatting in condemned buildings, sleeping on dirty old mattresses. From what I can tell, about the only things you own are that notebook of yours and the clothes on your back. And Powers, your son? He hates you and wants nothing more than to put you behind bars for the rest of your unnatural life, but as far as I can tell, he's still the closest thing to family or friends you have in this world."

I shifted in my seat and continued nursing my drink.

"If you intend for me to start working for you," I said with a slight slur, "being a prick about it is hardly a way to start. Flies and honey, remember?"

"This lifestyle of yours, the apparent vow of poverty and isolation from other people: I think somehow it's your way of paying penance for something you've done. Maybe it's just collective guilt from all the unwed mothers you've run out on. Or maybe it's something much worse, something that you can never forgive yourself for, no matter how long you live."

I glared at him.

"Oh, you have me all figured out then, Riley? You think you know who I am? Well then please, inform me, because I would love to hear about it. And if you hadn't picked up on it yet, that was a bit of sarcasm just there, you sanctimonious old walrus. I live on the barest of essentials because that's all I need, and it's all I want. That's a rare and precious quality in men, to be satisfied with nothing. And I live on my own because people just come with needless drama, and I don't have the patience for it anymore."

I leaned forward in my seat and pointed an accusing finger at him, or at least in his general direction.

"Do you have any clue how long I've been doing this? How many lives I've lived, and how fucked up every one of them has been? You don't have a fucking clue about me! Nobody does. You want to know who I am? I'm fucking nobody, and that's all I want to be. I've seen enough of humanity by now to know better than anyone else: people are shit. Greedy, cowardly, heartless, spiteful little piles of shit. That's why society is shit. Poverty, abuse, starvation, bigotry, xenophobia: it's all built into the system, from the foundations up. It's in our genes. It's even written into The Code.

"That's what I had to learn the hard way. Cutting the heads off the fucking hydra didn't do anything. It's not just a handful of 'evil' people at the top ruining things for everyone else. *Everybody* is shit, even you, even me. *Especially* me. And since I can never find the nerve to just off myself and be done with it, the best I can hope for is to just be nobody, sitting in the darkness, divorced from society, just killing time until doomsday. At least that way maybe people will finally leave me the fuck alone."

Riley took a long breath, then sighed and shook his head.

"I don't think you're as much of a misanthrope as you claim to be," he said. "And while you might have lived longer than most, you're not some kind of ancient immortal. You're just a man. Maybe a seriously disturbed man, but still a man. Deep down, you might even be a good one."

I surprised myself by laughing a bit at that, and tried to straighten up a bit. I leaned on my elbow and stared daggers at Riley. Our eyes remained fixed on one another, sitting in silence for several seconds. I started becoming conscious of just how far out of the stable that wild bucking bronco of a drunken rant had gotten. I'd said far more than I'd meant to. I'd gotten so perturbed and inebriated, my verbal affectations had started to slip as well.

"A good man... My dear Chief Riley, if that is truly what you believe, then you know even less about me than I thought. Maybe in time you'll come to appreciate that."

I finished off my glass for the final time and set it on the edge of the desk.

"Thanks for the drink."

I tipped my hat to him, then vanished back into the æther. I slid through the outside-facing wall and swooped up into the sky. As I picked up speed, the muted landscape below blurred together into an endless ocean of gray.

Epilogue

"What a terrible predicament this is. Here we are, forced out of our home, and for what reason? It was only a bit of fun, after all.

That treacherous girl Vivian. I warned you, did I not? I insisted it was foolish to trust her.

She seemed like such a nice girl. I thought we were friends. Why would she betray us this way? I simply cannot understand it.

She should be punished, for giving up our secrets, and for bringing that unscrupulous detective into our home and forcing us out into the cold. A simple curse will not do, I dare say.

I concur. While I liked Vivian as much as you did, Madam, we remain in peril as long as she and this detective know of us. Even after we find a new home, they will pose a threat to our peaceful lives.

I understand your concerns, gentlemen. Vivian will be dealt with in time. But don't forget who first threw our peaceful home into disarray in the first place. It is he who still poses the greatest threat.

Ah, but of course! That fiend! The embarrassment Sir Calvin and I were met with at his hands still fills me with contempt.

Madam, I must question pursuing him further. Did he not give a clear warning? It would seem he does not wish to play any longer.

He chose to join in, and he hasn't played fair since he began. He needs to be punished like anyone else. We won't forgive him for what he has done. We can't forgive him..."

"Hortensia?"

"Yes, momma?"

"Come on, baby. It's time to put away your toys and get ready for bed. You have school in the morning."

"Okay, momma."

The story will continue in:

The Mage's Code

book 02: escalate